The Secret Files of
Donald J. Trump

The Secret Files of Donald J. Trump
Vol. 1: The Tijuana Tango

A satirical dystopia

by
Francis le Lapin

A Black Coat Press Book

ISBN 978-1-61227-965-7. First Printing: April 2020. Published by Black Coat Press, an imprint of Hollywood Com-
ics.com, LLC, P.O. Box 17270, Encino, CA 91416. All rights
reserved. Except for review purposes, no part of this book may
be reproduced or transmitted in any form or by any means,
electronic or mechanical, including photocopying, recording,
or by any information storage and retrieval system, without
permission in writing from the publisher. The stories and
characters depicted in this novel are entirely fictional. Printed
in the United States of America.

Foreword

"Because he is such a comic-book character!"

That was Francis le Lapin's answer when I asked him why he had chosen to make the 45th President of the United States into the facsimile, avatar hero of his novel, which is primarily an exercise in alternative history, a genre that, in France, is often called "*uchronia*."

The word was coined by French philosopher Charles Renouvier (1815-1903), who published a book entitled *Uchronie, Utopie dans l'histoire* [*Uchronia: Utopia in History*] in 1857. "*Uchronia*" is, therefore, a 19th century neologism based on the model of the word "Utopia," itself created in 1516 by Thomas Moore to serve as the title for his famous eponymous book, Utopia), with "chronos" (time) instead of "topos" (place), hence meaning "non-time," a time that does not exist.

Uchronia works on a simple, even trivial principle: it starts with the question "What if...?" and applies it to the past. With it, it is possible to remake the world, to rewrite history. What if Napoleon hadn't lost at Waterloo? What if Hitler had joined the Vienna School of Fine Arts? What if General de Gaulle had been assassinated? What would the results have been? This speculative play with reality can, of course, be only fictional, since real history cannot be modified.

The first published uchronia is *Napoléon et la conquête du monde, 1812-1832, Histoire de la monarchie universelle,* initially published anonymously

5

in 1836. A second edition was published in 1841, bearing the title *Napoléon Apocryphe* and the signature Louis Geoffroy, and a third appeared in 1851, after the election of Louis-Napoleon—the future Emperor Napoleon III—as president of the Third French Republic. It was "rediscovered" in 1896, and has been regularly reprinted ever since.[1]

Geoffroy determined a precise point of divergence (Napoleon's decision to go on to Saint Petersburg instead of staying in Moscow) before rewriting history according to it (in it Napoleon conquers the world). He even jokingly inserts two references to our own history, when a fictional pamphlet, which actually retells history, as it really happened, is banned, and when Napoleon feels compelled, for no apparent reason, to destroy the island of Saint Helena.

What is the point of creating such chimera? Those who write alternative histories usually pursue a specific agenda. Military personnel use it to investigate the causes of a defeat and learn tactical lessons. Historians question the way events are connected. Writers like Philip K. Dick, the author of the Hugo award-winning *Man in the High Castle*, or Stephen King with *22/11/63*, use it to criticize the time in which they live, or alert us to a perceived danger by proposing a contemporary alternative, be it a utopian or a dystopian society.

When Uchronia is freed from the constraints of historical plausibility, its playful dimension allows it to open up the field of possibilities. Alan Moore and Dave Gibbons' *Watchmen*, Norman Spinrad's *The Iron Dream* or Michael Moorcock's *Gloriana*, to name but three gen-

---

[1] Black Coat Press, 2016, *The Apocryphal Napoléon,* translated by Brian Stableford (ISBN 978-1-61227-579-6).

re classics, are more fantastic because they moved away from the need for historical plausibility. These "uchronauts" fed on history to better betray it, but above all, to offer it a much larger and more eccentric playing field. Their works borrow from time travel, adventure stories, detective stories, fantasy, super-heroes, etc.

In *The Secret Files of Donald J. Trump*, Francis le Lapin borrows a page from Louis Geoffroy, but instead of Napoleon I, chooses the defeat—turned into a victory—of his nephew, Emperor Napoleon III, at the battle of Sedan against the Germans in September 1870. As le Lapin explains himself in his brief introduction, what if… Napoleon III, instead of being a spectacular failure, had proved to be an overwhelming success?

Which brings us back to Donald Trump.

The book is obviously a satire, but because it takes place on an entirely fictional world, and furthermore, in that world's past—1968—it has little relevance to whatever political challenges the real Donald Trump, and indeed the United States of America, face today.

"Because he is such a comic-book character!" said le Lapin.

Since the election of Ronald Reagan in 1980 as 40th President of the United States, the figure of the President, which was always elevated and held in awe throughout the world because of the tremendous power of the United States, has, for better or worse, become the topic of caricatural portrayals, as if that election had opened some mysterious floodgate in the collective unconscious.

Even though real-life comedian Coluche toyed with the notion of running for the French presidency in 1980, I know of no French work of fiction that deals with what if he had, and had won. On the other hand, Frank Miller portrayed a senile Reagan in his classic *The Dark Knight Returns*, Alan Moore had a President Robert Redford elected in *Watchmen*, and at one point, Superman's foe, Lex Luthor, was president in the DC Comics universe.

Such comic-bookish portrayals are not always negative: Harrison Ford in the movie *Air Force One* and Bill Pullman in *Independence Day* play presidents who are not unlike Francis le Lapin's hero (who, let us remember, is not yet president and, on his world, may never be) and owe more to James Bond than they do to Martin Sheen's Jed Bartlet. And let's not even consider *Abraham Lincoln, Vampire Hunter* which, by comparison, makes le Lapin's uchronic novel look quasi-historical!

"Francis le Lapin" is the nom-de-plume of a renowned Belgian writer born in Namur in 1947, who was once the editor-in-chief of the popular children's magazine *Le Fureteur* (1959-69), and also the author of several French comics and YA novels.

Feeling somewhat neglected today, he was sitting rather forlornly behind his table at the 2016 Sèvres sci-fi & fantasy festival when I first met him. He was signing a few of his books when I asked him if he had any unpublished manuscripts in a drawer that our French sister company, Rivière Blanche, might publish.

As it turned out, he didn't, but, one thing leading to another, he offered to write an entirely new novel—this book—his first written directly in English (with editing by Randy).

I hope you will enjoy it as much as I did, and celebrate the return of one of my favorite authors from my childhood.

Jean-Marc Lofficier

Introduction

The world depicted in this novel diverged from ours when Emperor Napoleon III of France, instead of being a spectacular failure, proved to be an overwhelming success.

As a result, France did not lose Mexico in the 1860s and won the Battle of Sedan against Germany in 1870.

It remained a constitutional imperial monarchy and its political influence spread to include Germany and Austria to the East, Italy to the South, and Belgium to the North. England, the Netherlands, Spain, Denmark and the Baltics remained independent kingdoms.

In this world, Russia did not fall to the Bolshevik Revolution. Instead, it remained a Monarchy, and eventually became France's greatest enemy, leading to a single seven-year Great War starting in 1932 between the two competing super-powers, the "Western Alliance," which also included the United States, and the "Eastern Union," comprised of Russia, China, Korea and Japan. South America and Africa remained mostly uninvolved.

The Great War was fought in the trenches of Poland, the "North African theater" (Egypt) and the "Pacific theater." It was eventually won by the Western Alliance in 1939 when France built the first A-bomb, the power of which it demonstrated in the French Sahara.

After the Great War, France and England fought to keep their colonies, which led to a series of localized conflicts known as the Colonial Wars. Mexico, however, gained its independence and its own Empire expanded to include Central America, Colombia, Ecuador and Venezuela, Nevertheless, it remained tightly allied with France.

On this world, the United States are the equivalent of Brazil and Canada in ours—important, but a second-tier power. (Alaska is still Russian.) There is no state of Israel, but a proxy guerilla war has been fought in Lebanon by the great powers since the mid-1950s. And Japan retreated into a somewhat hostile, isolationist mode.

When our story begins—in 1968—the conquest of space is being handled by a French/British/American team based in Reggane, French Sahara, and a Russian/Chinese team based in Kazakhstan.

Francis le Lapin

CHAPTER I

At 8:12 p.m. on April 22, 1968, a warmly illuminated luxury train set off in silence, followed by the admiring glances of the people who, from other platforms, watched its departure.

The *Silver Arrow Express* bound for Mexico City via San Diego, Tijuana, Mexicali and Durango, left Los Angeles' Union Station with the powerful grace of a rocket. It crossed the suburbs of Orange County at eighty mph, and then, still accelerating, rushed into the night towards the American-Mexican border.

Just under two hours later, it stopped at the Chula Vista border point, where the Mexican imperial police and customs agents boarded it for the usual checks.

Comfortably seated in his window seat, Pavel Zakuski handed over his Russian passport without even looking at the official who, stamp in hand, was checking the passengers. He heard the slapping sound of the stamp on paper, took the passport back, and stored it in his jacket's inside pocket, then returned to reading his copy of the *Los Angeles Daily Examiner*.

The ritual question of the Mexican customs agent in his white and gold uniform asking him if he had anything to declare forced him to look up. He replied with a negative sign of his head. Because he was Russian, and obviously well-off, the officer took his word for it. Nevertheless, noticing a pocket-sized transistor radio on the table in front of Zakuski, the officer pointed at it and asked:

"Purchased in the United States?"

Zakuski's face lost its distant expression. The shadow of a smile appeared on his face as he replied:

"Why, yes. The proof of that is that it no longer works."

With anyone else, the customs agent would have laughed, but not with a Russian. While independent from France since the end of the Colonial War, the relationship between the Mexican and Russian Empires were still tense.

"Really?" the customs agent wondered. "May I?"

Zakuski gave an approving nod. The customs agent took the transistor radio and pressed the on-switch. Placing the speaker against his ear, he could only hear a slight hum. With his thumb, he turned the knob looking for any of the local stations, but received no signal.

"Maybe it's because the signals do not penetrate these new metallic cars?" said the officer, puzzled.

He opened the back of the radio.

"A brand new device like that should be working," he added.

"Yes—in theory," agreed Zakuski. "It is also possible that the battery is dead, having been stored too long."

The customs agent examined the inside of the radio, then closed it, and returned it to its owner.

"It is possible," he admitted. "It only takes a small thing. Good evening, *Señor*."

He moved on to the next passenger, and Zakuski went back to reading the *Daily Examiner*, freed from a sense of foreboding.

These days, the formalities of entry into the Mexican Empire were reduced to a minimum. No one expressed concern about the transistor radio, the free circulation of which was now tolerated in Mexico, like that of standard cameras.

Fifteen minutes later, the *Silver Arrow* entered the station in Tijuana. Zakuski took his tweed overcoat from the rack where he had hung it, put it on, and shoved the radio in its pocket. Carrying a single leather suitcase, he got off the train and mingled with the other passengers walking towards the exit.

Strolling towards the center of town, he walked by the Cathedral de Nuestra Señora de Guadalupe, the bell tower of which was outlined in black against the halo cast by hundreds of city lights. There, he hailed a cab.

"Calle del General Forey," he told the driver. "I can't tell you the number, but it's just outside the city limit. I'll guide you."

The cab took a wide boulevard that described a quarter of a circle then, turning right, traveled down a long avenue lined with modern high-rise buildings.

At the next crossroad, it turned into a maze of smaller streets. After a quarter of an hour, it arrived at what looked like an industrial zone, where factories were spaced out in seemingly random order and residential houses were rare.

After another ten minutes, Zakuski ordered the driver to stop at an intersection. He paid for the ride with a stack of Mexican Francs, leaving a handsome tip, then stepped out of the cab.

Before the driver had completed its round turn, Zakuski had already disappeared from the area illuminated by the streetlights and vanished into the surrounding darkness.

It would have been hard to find a better place to conduct secret business, especially at this time of night.

While strolling in a deserted street along the darkness, not being able to see more than ten paces ahead, Zakuski was already missing the warm comfort of the train ride, although the temperature was, in fact, rather mild for the season.

He finally reached the agreed-upon meeting point: a shed with a corrugated metal roof, open to the wind, in which a bunch of barrels had been stored in pyramidal form. At the precise moment when the Russian was preparing to hide behind one of them, the headlights of a car coming from the other end of the road struck him. The powerful beam then moved, sweeping the industrial wasteland before again shining straight at the hangar, indicating the car was parking.

Zakuski's silhouette, fleetingly lit, disappeared behind the pile of metal drums. He had not tried to conceal himself, guessing that the car belonged to the man he was there to meet.

The vehicle's lights went out. Darkness returned to the shed.

Zakuski took off his overcoat, folded it and put it on top of his suitcase. He heard a car door slam, and prepared to meet Requesón.

The driver stepped closer. When he was less than five feet away, Zakuski stared in shock, his nerves shattered, because the man was not Requesón!

The expressionless face of the newcomer was completely indecipherable. With lightning speed, he pulled a gun from his pocket and used it to strike a glancing blow to Zakuski's left temple.

Mouth open, eyes tightly shut, the Russian crumpled into a ball as he collapsed to the ground.

He had had enough time to be afraid, but not to understand what had happened to him.

CHAPTER II

Five days later, Donald J. Trump pulled out of his underground garage in Brooklyn and drove his black imported De Dion-Bouton Papillon towards Brighton Beach.

He parked on Coney Island Avenue, as usual, and walked down to the *Little Odessa* restaurant where he usually met his Russian handler, Boris Fedorovitch Stroganoff of the Okhrana, the nickname of the Department for Protecting the Public Security and Order of the Russian Empire.

When he entered the back room where the two usually met, Trump immediately saw that the older man was in a foul mood.

Stroganoff was in his sixties, overweight, and nearly bald. His always grumpy face was highlighted by a thick, ill-kempt, grey mustache. His horn-rimmed glasses were permanently askew, and he liked to chew on the end of an old, dirty, ivory cigarette-holder, that currently held an unlit cigarette.

On the table before him were enough dishes to qualify as a small banquet.

Trump hung his coat on a peg. Upon sitting down across from the Russian, he noticed with delight that the restaurant had finally replaced their rickety old chairs.

He lodged his two hundred and two pound body onto the new chrome tubed seat, thinking that *Little Odessa* must be doing well.

"You're late," said Stroganoff gruffly, making a gesture inviting his agent to partake in the bounty. "When I call you, it is *always* urgent, you should know that."

Trump helped himself to copious servings of several dishes, ignoring the ominous warnings of a growing pot belly. As a matter of fact, he had received the call only one hour and thirty-five minutes ago exactly.

"Excuse me if I had to swallow what I had in my mouth before coming here," he hissed in a tone venomous enough to prove that any command from Stroganoff left him cold.

"Don't be insolent," enjoined the Russian. "You know how much you owe us. Without us, you'd be in a debtor's prison, disowned by your own father."

This time, there was no repartee.

Trump had begun working for the Russians two years earlier, after one of his real estate ventures had turned sour. Scrambling for money, he had been only too happy to see the Russians invest in his failed casino project and keep it afloat. More than anything else, he feared the opprobrium that he would have received from his father, Fred C. Trump, had he been forced to confess his failure.

Since then, he had taken a liking to helping the Russians; it titillated his ego and made him—at least in his own eyes—feel like an "international man of mystery." The more prosaic truth was that, far from being a "mystery," his sideline business was well known to the authorities. However, they didn't really care as long as his activities were not directed against the United States.

Fred C. Trump, who didn't have a very high opinion of his son, had been pleasantly surprised to see new money coming in, and Donald, in exchange for tidbits of intelligence about his extracurricular activities, had been able to keep Uncle Sam off their backs; so everyone was happy.

Stroganoff opened and closed six folders that were lying next to him on the bench, no longer remembering which one was the one dealing with the matter at hand. Then, apparently outraged by this new manifestation of the law of universal vexation, he resolved to forget the documents he had been seeking and began in a more conciliatory tone:

"No hard feelings, Donald, eh?" he asked.

"None at all. I'm a big man. Do you need a light?" said Trump, pulling out a gold-plated lighter.

Stroganoff looked at him sharply, searching for some hidden meaning, but realized that it was only his unlit cigarette that had prompted Trump to make the offer.

"No, thank you," he grumbled while feeling his pockets, without succeeding in reaching his own lighter.

Sighing, he allowed Trump to relight his cigarette and puffed on it hard, creating a huge cloud of smoke before finally addressing the matter at hand, albeit in his usual convoluted way:

"It is rare when people in our business receive gifts," he growled, leaning against the back of his seat, his hands flat on the table. "But when that happens, I always wonder about the intentions of the giver
..."

Trump also smoked—although he'd thought about quitting—and lit a *Gitane,* pulled from a silver-plated case he kept in the left pocket of his jacket.

"Someone sent you a box of chocolates?" he asked sarcastically, while swallowing a blini.

"You're not entirely wrong," replied the Russian, "in the sense that this also weighs heavily on my stomach. Guess who the sender is?"

"Lady Godiva?"

"No. The French Consulate in Los Angeles."

Trump raised a curious eyebrow.

"The French? Really?" he asked.

"They had a small package delivered to our own Consulate, with an accompanying note that said, in effect, 'We think this belongs to you. Best regards.' The package contained a small transistor radio of the type you can buy anywhere. It presented only one peculiarity: it didn't work."

A wisp of smoke escaped from Trump's lips, his features now reflecting his full attention.

"Diplomats can sometimes be clever too, so the L.A. Consulate fobbed the radio off on us, perhaps to avoid blame just in case it turned out to be something important," continued Stroganoff with a shade of sarcasm. "You do know that we have a rather sophisticated lab here?"

"It's common knowledge," said Trump. "Even the FBI knows it. And, what did you discover inside that transistor radio?"

Gloomily, the Russian replied while Trump continued wolfing down the food:

"Something that should not have been there. Wait, I'll show you…"

Stroganoff again dived into his pile of brown folders until he found the right one. It contained a report and a couple of photographs showing a tiny oval object, about eight by five millimeters, in the shape of a small tower glued to a square, with three wires as thin as strands of hairs coming from it.

"What is it?" Trump asked, after looking at the photos.

"Our scientists call it a rhodion transistor; it's some kind of new, advanced transistor, with a performance vastly superior to those using germanium crystals, especially in the higher frequencies, or so I'm told. It's a new Russian invention..."

"Is it a military secret?"

"Well, no... It's being licensed for a variety of industrial applications, including a new type of radar."

"So?" Trump said. "Where's the problem?"

"This is precisely what I asked myself," replied Stroganoff. "The French are known for their Machiavellian minds. What is their purpose in sending us this device?"

"To have a little fun at your expense?" volunteered Trump. "A way of saying, 'we had it, we broke it, sorry'?"

Stroganoff waved off the comment.

"No, that would be contrary to all the rules of our profession. You don't notify your opponent of a successfully conducted operation, even if, as would be the case here, it was a waste of time. I'm more inclined to see it as some kind of warning, like, 'Beware, someone is stealing your technology, but we want you to know that we are not involved.' This seems to me more consistent with their current desire for *détente*."

Trump thought about this for two seconds, took another mouthful of beef blinchiki, then objected:

"Unless we—the Americans—stole it. The French know it, and by giving it back to us, they hope to trigger an investigation that would ultimately result in creating a quarrel with the U.S. After all, it wouldn't be the first time the FBI or the CIA messed up."

Stroganoff did not reject that possibility out of hand.

"That would be diabolical," he admitted, "but not impossible. So, now you see why I'd like to know where we stand. Since the French passed this ball to us, we're going to run with it, even at the risk of playing the cards they dealt us," he concluded, mixing his metaphors.

Trump took a last puff of his *Gitane* before crushing it in the ashtray. Now he knew why Stroganoff had summoned him.

"You want me to try to get some information from the French Consulate in Los Angeles?"

"Yes. You know the French and their psychology. Plus, your family has some real estate investments in California. Tell them we 're touched by their gesture, we deeply appreciate their cooperation, etc., etc., but ask them how they came to be in possession of the device, and who stole it in the first place."

"Sounds good," replied Trump. "But I'm skeptical. If the French didn't want us to untangle this by ourselves, they would have included more information with the shipment."

The Russian spymaster displayed his crafty smile.

"Not necessarily, because, in that case, they wouldn't know if we'd bit or not. Since they clearly have some objective in mind, they must be waiting for our reaction. And the best way for them to find out was to provide us with too little information."

"If you're right, they should receive me with open arms," said Trump, getting up. "Do you have a name for me to talk to?"

Stroganoff took out another folder and looked inside

"Yes. Ask for the Military Attaché... Colonel Roquefort... Here's a letter of introduction that designates you as a consultant to our Russian-American Trade Delegation. They won't be fooled, of course, but we must maintain appearances."

Trump took the sheet of paper, folded it in four, and pocketed it.

"When should I go?"

"The sooner, the better."

"How should I play it?"

Stroganoff pushed his glasses back higher on his nose.

"Be reserved, but forceful enough to make them believe we care about this. Between the two of us, I don't really... The discovery of the rhodion transistor was published in scientific journals, with its principles and its design. We even released photos. However, this should not be taken as an open invitation to let everyone and their neighbor copy it. That little gadget is too rich in opportunities to let it be duplicated before we have even started producing it in mass quantities."

While putting on his overcoat, Trump said:

"In essence, the thief—whoever he is—has stolen something that will soon be on the open market?"

"Correct. And this can be interpreted in two ways: either he misunderstood its intrinsic value..." Stroganoff paused to better articulate his thoughts. "...Or he is very anxious to use it for an application that he wants to be the first to develop."

"Something you guys haven't thought of?"

"Yes. One thing is certain, however. This involves both the Americans and the Mexicans, who may or may not be a convenient proxy for the French. We don't know yet. But the fact that, in order to cross the border undetected, they hid the rhodion inside a disabled transistor radio speaks volumes. No pun intended."

Trump pursed his lips and said:

"It stinks of a private network, don't you think?"

"You may well be right. The CIA, if they're involved, would have microfilmed the designs, not stolen a prototype to be reverse engineered later. Nevertheless, I want to clarify who did it—and why."

Trump left without paying. He never did. That's one of the things he liked best about being a Russian asset.

CHAPTER III

The French Consulate in Los Angeles occupied four floors in a handsome multi-storied white building on Sunset Boulevard, at the edge of Beverly Hills.

After having presented his credentials, Donald J. Trump was led into the office of the Military Attaché by a security guard. He was a man of about forty-five years-old, strongly built, dressed in a dark blue pinstripe suit despite his military rank.

Portraits of Emperor Napoleon VII and the powerful Marshall de Gaulle hung on the wall. The Attaché received his visitor affably.

"I am Colonel Roquefort. Nice to meet you, Mr. Trump.:

He spoke in perfect English.

"I am honored, Colonel," Trump said in somewhat approximate French. "First of all, let me thank you for your gift. Your kind gesture was appreciated by those in high places."

Roquefort raised his hand in a typical Gallic gesture.

"The return of a lost object to its rightful owner does not deserve so much praise," he said with an ambiguous smile. "To act otherwise would have been inappropriate."

Considering the circumstances, it was clear that Colonel Roquefort lacked neither style nor humor.

"You can understand that the receipt of this transistor radio has aroused our curiosity," Trump said in a light tone. "Would it be indiscreet to ask you by which fortunate circumstances this item fell into your hands?"

Roquefort's smile disappeared and his face suddenly grew concerned.

"Sadly, I'm not able to give you many details in this regard," he lied, without looking his visitor in the eyes.

"The recovery of this device would lose much of its value if we were to ignore how it disappeared in the first place," argued Trump. "I presume you wouldn't have returned the item in question if you were determined to hide the identity of the thief."

The colonel looked up, and his clear gaze fixed on Trump.

"Let's not confuse issues," he said, steepling his fingers. "Who had the device in his possession is one thing; how he obtained it is another; and to tell you how we learned of it is a third. I can tell you about the first point, but cannot enlighten you about the other two."

"Cannot" in this instance meant "would not" as Trump construed it.

"My Russian principals would be delighted if you could at least throw some light on the first point," he asserted. "Although this leak might not be of major importance to them, I think they'd like to prevent another indiscretion, possibly by a member of their own laboratories."

"I quite understand," Roquefort said approvingly. "This is what I can tell you: this transistor radio belonged to a person of Russian nationality called Pavel Zakuski. He died in a road accident a week ago in Tijuana. According to the Mexican authorities, he was run over by a car at night."

Trump did not think it appropriate to mention that this story appeared rather unbelievable on the face of it.

"Are you certain of his name?" he asked.

"It was the name on his passport," replied the colonel, indicating that he wasn't ready to vouch for anything else.

"Do you have the passport?"

"No. The Mexican police kept it. Their inquiries aren't yet over."

Trump nodded thoughtfully. Roquefort was spinning like a top. The only disclosure that seemed reliable was the name—Pavel Zakuski. As for the rest...

"I won't impose on your generosity any further," he said, preparing to leave. "All's well that ends well, it seems: Pavel Zakuski is now dead and buried, and likely took his secret to the grave. My principals will be happy. Good-bye, Colonel, and thank you again."

Forty minutes later, Donald J. Trump walked into his office located on the 35th floor of the Sberbank Tower in Downtown Los Angeles. Sberbank was the largest Russian bank, having been established through a decree by Tsar Nikolai I in 1841. The tower also housed the Russian Consulate, which was more than convenient.

Once behind his desk, Trump immediately called Stroganoff.

"So?" inquired the Russian spymaster.

"Mostly a wild goose chase," replied Trump, summing up. "The man who was in possession of your rhodion transistor was, it seems, a Russian named Pavel

Zakuski. He was killed in a traffic accident in Tijuana. As a stupendous coincidence, a French agent was passing nearby just at the right time to relieve him of his radio..."

Stroganoff also appeared to find this "coincidence" hilarious.

"How lucky for them!" he snickered. Then, more seriously, he added: "Roquefort didn't tell you why they were after this Zakuski *moujik*?"

"He was both direct and evasive," Trump clarified. "He clearly indicated that the details behind this affair were none of our business. In return, I made it clear that, with Zakuski being Russian, and dead, you no longer had much interest in the case."

"I'm certain he didn't believe you, but that doesn't matter: it may encourage them to give us some more information one of these days."

"What have you decided?" Trump asked with a familiarity born of two years of collaboration.

"I have decided nothing," replied Stroganoff. "Or rather, I have decided to entrust the next steps to your own initiative. It will be a great exercise for you. Open this Pandora's box and see what flies out."

Trump reflected for a minute.

"Don't you think it's strange that the French want us to investigate this rather than doing it themselves?"

"Yes, it is," replied the Russian. "And I'm more curious about that than the theft of the rhodion itself. It looks to me as if they don't want *to get wet*, as they say."

"What is your *real* interest here, Stroganoff? Identifying the person behind this, or our Gallic friends' true purpose?"

"Both, Donald, both! Elucidate the first and it shall shed light on the second!"

"From where I sit, it looks as if you're OK with the French eating the chestnuts that I'm going to pull out of the fire."

"True, true," agreed the Russian with undisturbed serenity. "But what kind of chestnuts you will pull out remains to be seen, Donald. *Dasvidaniya.*"

CHAPTER IV

Donald J. Trump launched his investigation in the laziest way possible: he called his attorney, Ellis J. Whitestone. Whitestone had his contacts in the local FBI office check on Pavel Zakuski.

The next day, he received substantial and valuable information.

Zakuski was, indeed, a Russian citizen, but with dual American citizenship. He was the Senior Representative for the Western United States of the powerful Russian firm *Novosibirsk Optiko-Mechanicheskoye Obyedinenie* (Novosibirsk Optical & Mechanical Enterprise, or NOMO), which specialized in precision optics and the manufacturing of cameras. He owned a condo in Hollywood. He traveled widely, and made frequent trips to Russia. The American authorities had never found anything suspicious about any of his activities.

And, noted Trump, the FBI did not seem to be aware of his recent death.

Pavel Zakuski had obviously had been engaged in an illegal operation involving spies working in both Russia and the United States alongside his commercial activities. A visit to his home was clearly in order.

At 10 p.m., Donald J. Trump arrived in Hollywood. Night was falling on Los Angeles when he parked his car on Wilshire Boulevard.

He watched with curiosity as the patrons entered and left a popular eatery, where a small crowd of onlookers were also staked out, anxious to catch even a fleeting glimpse of a celebrity.

On foot, he turned onto the nearest street and walked uphill for a couple of blocks. Zakuski's condo was in an average, four-storied brown building, with parking to one side, surrounded by ordinary houses, all shrouded in the diffuse glow of the parsimonious street lights.

It wasn't surprising that a foreign businessman, single, would choose to live in this area; it was as nondescript as possible, totally lacking in charm.

Trump entered the building by picking the lock. A quick check in the mailbox bearing Zakuski's name showed that it was empty, except for a couple of advertising flyers.

Trump hated stairs and was already exhausted from his brief walk, so he took the elevator up to the fourth floor. Arriving in front of Zakuski's door, he rang the bell, just in case. After all, the Russian might not have been living alone...

No one answered, so he examined the lock and began to pick it, too. On the fifth try, he succeeded and entered the condo. His short groping fingers touched a switch on the wall and he turned on the lights. Through the large glass window in front of him, he could see the panorama of Hollywood, studded with thousands of points of light.

The living room was large, with bare walls. It contained a great quantity of the equipment that Zakuski must have used for demonstrations to his clients: enlargers, a projector, two or three cameras, tripods, a pearly white screen, a telescope, and other optical and camera accessories.

Trump thought that this wasn't where he was likely to find any clues about Zakuski's illegal activities. He decided to visit the other rooms.

A hallway opened to the right of the living room/workshop, leading to two bedrooms and a separate office which could be accessed by a few steps. The latter contained a desk, two filing cabinets, and could be converted into a third bedroom with a fold-out sofa bed.

Trump started searching the place, top to bottom. His task was made easier by the fact that nothing was locked.

He found export licenses, invoices, order books, letters in both English and Russian, in short, typical business documents that appeared to be legitimate, but would require a lengthier analysis. He photographed the correspondence. He became convinced that Zakuski, when he had left the condo, hadn't believed he'd be away for long, as unopened mail still lay on the desk's in-tray.

After a thorough search, Trump had not gotten hold of the slightest evidence that proved that Pavel Zakuski was anything other than what he appeared to be.

He then returned to the living room/workshop, wondering if he had failed to detect a hidden place where the Russian might have concealed more important papers. His meticulous exploration led him to the balcony where, near the railing, he saw a garden table on which sat an electric iron. There was also a telescope pointed towards the rooftops of Hollywood, mounted on a tripod.

This unusual item drew Trump's attention. He took a closer look at the telescope. Unlike a conventional optical instrument, both of its ends terminated with the same size lenses. In addition, one of them was opaque: it looked like the milky screen of a television set.

This strange lens faced the side where normally an observer would sit to look at closer views of the city, but in this case, he would have been unable to see anything.

Trump finally realized the true nature of the device when he noticed an electric cord leading from the "telescope" to a plug lying on the ground, near a power outlet in the wall. He plugged it in, eager to see if his guess was correct.

After a few seconds, the milky lens lost its opacity and became darker.

Trump put an eye to the "telescope" and, immediately, saw a very different view from that which would have been provided by an ordinary telescope. The instrument did provide a high magnification, but his vision was of strangely contrasted rooftops, streets and buildings.

The a/c units formed bright spots, the electric lights had a diminished luster, and the hoods of the cars appeared brighter than their headlights...

It did not take a rocket scientist to deduce that the device was infrared-sensitive,

Trump turned it off. He wondered what kind of person would be interested in such a thing. Was it something Zakuski sold to his customers? In war time, such instruments could be very useful, especially for nighttime combat, but Southern California was not a battlefield...

Unless... Trump almost shouted as he understood: the U.S. Navy had used infrared optical signaling because its radiation, invisible to the naked eye, could pierce any fog, and guaranteed absolute secrecy in short-range communications.

So why wouldn't spies use the same devices to communicate within a city?

The location of this condo, overlooking Hollywood, with the business district not far away, strengthened his hypothesis.

But if the infrared "telescope" was used by Zakuski to receive secret messages, what did he use to send them?

Trump was seized with a sudden urge to laugh. The emitting source of infrared radiation had been in front of him all along: the electric iron! Seven hundred and fifty watts of electrical energy converted into heat radiation by the simplest method ever invented!

The iron and the "telescope" were the equivalent of the microphone and earpiece of a wireless radio!

After a short period of euphoria, Trump had to admit that this discovery was not in and of itself a breakthrough. That Zakuski was in touch with other spies was to be expected. But as their mode of communication totally preserved their anonymity, there was no reason to gloat just yet—especially if the news of his death had already been discovered by his network, a very real possibility.

Trump finished his inspection, looking carefully at every device stored in the workshop/living room. He wondered if he should ask Stroganoff to send a forensic team for a more thorough examination, or, instead, turn it into a mousetrap for Zakuski's mysterious associates?

He resolved to discuss it with the Russian spymaster the next morning, and to ask that a few Okhrana agents be assigned to monitor the condo.

He turned off the lights, closed and relocked the door behind him, and left. His mind busy with his latest findings, he took the elevator down.

As he reached the ground floor, another man stepped into the elevator just as Trump walked out. The two men nodded to each other, with indifferent glances.

Trump went on his way, while the elevator went back up.

Out on the street, he stopped. Something had tickled his subconscious. He would have bet a large sum of money that the person whom he had just met was Russian.

Relying more on intuition than on any logical reasoning, Trump turned back silently and reentered the building.

Judging from the indicator lights, the elevator had already reached the third floor, and its ascent continued. It stopped on the fourth floor.

Trump hated taking stairs, but this time, he had no choice. As stealthily as he could, he climbed them, two steps at a time, until he arrived, somewhat out of breath, at the apartment the late Zakuski had occupied.

The door had not been forced open, and there was light coming from beneath it.

Someone who was able to enter Zakuski's condo with his own key deserved special attention.

Judging by the sounds, the mysterious visitor was not taking any precautions. Trump heard him pacing through the workshop/living room, moving equipment.

Then he must have gone into the office or one of the bedrooms because his movements became inaudible.

Shortly after, he returned to the living room.

Trump suddenly opened the door with his left hand. In his right, he held an automatic pistol.

Seeing him, the man started in shock.

CHAPTER V

"Chto? Gosha!" uttered the bewildered man in Russian.

He put his hands up as if they were pulled by invisible strings.

His gun still pointed at the visitor, Donald J. Trump closed the door and leaned against it.

"What are you doing here?" he asked in a low voice. "Do you have business with Pavel Zakuski?"

"Da… Yes," replied the visitor, still distraught.

He had a lean face with sharp features, and hollow cheeks darkened with stubble. This was the face of prematurely aged man. Gray eyes, graying eyebrows. He was dressed in an overcoat a little too long for him.

"Turn around," ordered Trump.

The man complied.

Trump approached him. Keeping his automatic pressed to his hip, and placing himself at a slight angle, he felt his prisoner's clothes, the back pocket, underarm and inner pockets.

Then, stepping back, he continued:

"OK, you can face me now. Lower your hands."

Docile, the Russian spun around and looked back anxiously.

"So what's your business with Zakuski? Why are you here?" asked Trump sharply.

The visitor quickly licked his thin lips.

"I... I have a job to do... I take care of all this equipment..."

Using both hands, he pointed at the devices scattered around him.

"Why?"

"I am technician from *Novosibirsk Optiko-Mechanichesckoye Obyedinenie.* Mr. Zakuski was my boss. He died recently in traffic accident. But who are you?"

"You don't want to know. Show me some ID."

Stunned, the Russian withdrew his passport from his left pocket and handed it to Trump.

Without relinquishing his weapon, keeping the Russian in his sight from the corner of his eye, Trump quickly leafed through it.

Vladimir Poshekhonsky, born April 14, 1920, in Kiev. Occupation: engineer. The U.S. immigration stamp was dated from five years ago.

Trump gave him back the passport.

"What's your local address?"

"Westlake Apartments, on Cahuenga."

"Do you have any ID showing that you work for NOMO?"

"*Da...* My business cards," offered Poshekhonsky, ready to show one.

"That doesn't prove much. A letter of employment or some kind of company ID would be better."

Poshekhonsky's attitude betrayed his embarrassment.

"*Nyet...* I have nothing on me like that... Wait! Yes! I have invoice for five cameras to store in Beverly Hills on our company's letterhead. Now I have to go deliver them, since Mr. Zakuski..."

He pulled out a letter printed on blue paper with NOMO letterhead, addressed to a store on Rodeo Drive.

Trump examined the invoice, considering it an acceptable reference.

"Who told you Zakuski was dead?" he asked.

Poshekhonsky seemed to find the question surprising.

"Ah... Louie Ragusano, our plant manager."

"You have a plant here?"

"*Da*. In Burbank. The components are manufactured in Russia, but for some special custom order, they have to be assembled here, and there's always need for... how do you say?... fine-tuning. That's what I do—the fine-tuning," he added, smiling.

"And how did this Louie get the news?"

"I do not know. I think a policeman came to tell him that Zakuski had fatal accident in Tijuana."

"Why did you come here?"

"Louie asked me to come and collect all of Zakuski's business papers and equipment, what he kept at home, and bring back to plant. We're waiting for Novosibirsk to appoint successor. I also have to contact all major customers and ask them to send orders directly to Louie for the time being."

Poshekhonsky's explanations rang true, but his apparent sincerity did not necessarily mean that he was unaware of his late boss' clandestine activities.

"What was Zakuski doing in Tijuana?" Trump asked harshly.

Poshekhonsky's furrowed features expressed the greatest perplexity.

"I do not know," he sighed. "Louie was very surprised to learn that he had died in Mexico. Mr. Zakuski had no real business reason to be there. Now, why you are asking me all these questions?"

There was a fifty-percent chance that Poshekhonsky was just a technician working for the Russian optic manufacturer and nothing more. But he also could be Zakuski's accomplice in his other activities...

Ignoring the other man's question, Trump said in a softened tone:

"Come with me. I'm responsible for securing the property of the deceased until his legal heirs show up. You have to complete an official statement and prove your rights, or you can't touch anything here."

Poshekhonsky visibly found the prospect unpleasant, and he replied irritably:

"This really necessary?"

Trump knew that it wasn't, but he had another objective in mind, so he stated with certainty:

"It's absolutely mandatory, Mr. Poshekhonsky. Please walk ahead of me..."

The two men left the apartment. While Trump relocked it, he asked:

"By the way, how come you've got a key to this place?"

"NOMO pays mortgage," Poshekhonsky explained. "We have double of all keys at office."

"Who chose this place?"

"Mr. Zakuski. He hated living in hotel. And the equipment had become too cumbersome to carry around."

As they went down the elevator. Trump continued his questioning:

"How long had he been working in Los Angeles?"

"Er... He was appointed in '64, if I remember correctly."

"When did he move in here?"

"About two years later... June '66, maybe?".

Trump and Poshekhonsky emerged onto the street. It was now a quarter past eleven. Ten minutes later, they got into Trump's car.

The Okhrana had a number of police officers on its payroll, and Stroganoff had told Trump that one of them, Captain Van Dijk, was posted at the West L.A. Station. That's where he decided to go.

Trump parked the car on Butler, and, dragging Poshekhonsky with him, went into the West L.A. Station. Using a prearranged codeword, he obtained an immediate interview with the Captain, during which he revealed in a few words the reason for his visit.

Van Dijk obligingly lent his help to the operation: Poshekhonsky was asked to tell why he had entered a private home without the written permission of its absent owner; in what capacity did he feel authorized to remove the high value devices that were stored in the condo; what did he intend to do with them; etc.

Meanwhile, in a nearby office, Trump called the Russian Embassy and demanded that four Okhrana agents be dispatched to watch the condo 24/7, and follow any person entering it, and capturing them if they tried to cross the US-Mexico border.

He also asked that another two agents be assigned to follow Vladimir Poshekhonsky, currently being questioned at the West L.A. police station, but who would be released in an hour or so.

Once this was done, Trump made use of the inter-phone to tell Captain Van Dijk to let Poshekhonsky go in about an hour, and to drag things out until then.

He then thanked the LAPD officer and left the station.

CHAPTER VI

The next day, Donald J. Trump called Boris Stroganoff to report on the progress of his investigation and the measures he had taken.

The Russian spymaster agreed that they shouldn't hinder Poshekhonsky's freedom of movement. The important thing was to learn whether he was part of Zakuski's network or not.

As for the possibilities of infrared communication between Zakuski and other parties, this was of particular interest to Stroganoff.

"If they only contact each other in this way, the security of their network must be close to absolute," he said in wonder.

"Yes," agreed Trump. "I can't imagine us—or the FBI—planting men equipped with infrared instruments on all the rooftops in Hollywood. Besides, how would they know where to aim? A few degrees off, and they'd totally miss the source of the infrared energy..."

"Yes, that would be impractical," admitted Stroganoff. "Maybe scopes with a larger field of vision? I'm not even sure they exist, except on board some of our naval vessels. No, we need to solve our problem some other way..."

"I agree," Trump said. "I thought I'd snoop around that factory in Burbank. Could you send me the rhodion specimen from Zakuski's transistor radio?"

"Yes. You'll have it in 48 hours, special delivery. What do you plan to do with it?"

"Zakuski had to get it, or steal it, from someone else," said Trump. "Since he hadn't gone back to Russia recently, our circle of suspects is limited, and probably located here, in Los Angeles."

"That's a good idea," agreed Stroganoff. "But until proven otherwise, this Poshekhonsky character may not be involved in any of this."

"Maybe; Zakuski was killed a week or so ago. If one of his accomplices was instructed to remove incriminating evidence from his condo, they would have had plenty of time to do it before I showed up."

"A French agent preceding you at the condo wouldn't surprise me at all," said Stroganoff. "But this still doesn't tell us why Roquefort dragged us into this affair…"

"Just to give you an ulcer," sneered Trump. "I'll call you as soon as I learn anything new. The agents I asked to keep an eye on the condo should stay in place for a few more days. I'll go back there after Poshekhonsky has removed the equipment."

"Why?"

"To see if he took the infrared telescope and the iron, or left them there."

"Why?"

"Because that telescope didn't have any factory markings. If Poshekhonsky removes it, that means it belonged to, NOMO. Then you could use your contacts with U.S. Customs to find out how many such devices entered California, who ordered them, and what their alleged purpose was."

Stroganoff could be heard sucking on his cigarette-holder before responding:

"Donald, you are really the best asset we've ever acquired   in   this   shithole   of   a   country."

CHAPTER VII

Two days later, at 11 a.m., Donald J. Trump showed up at the NOMO factory on Alameda in Burbank. It was a non-descript industrial building, without any outside markings.

After leaving his car in the visitor's parking lot, he asked a mousy blonde receptionist if he could talk to Louie Ragusano, the plant manager. He was then taken to a large, modern conference room.

After a few minutes, Ragusano arrived. He was a short, fat man, balding prematurely, and what remained of his hair was greasy and black. Trump explained that his father was planning to install a network of computerized cameras in a new high-security office building they were building for the U.S. government in Downtown Manhattan, and asked for the utmost discretion about the conversation they were about to have.

Intrigued, Ragusano gave him all the required assurances. Trump then took the rhodion transistor he had received earlier that morning from his pocket and placed it on the top of the glass table.

"In your opinion," he asked, "how many people working here might have had access to this device?"

Ragusano's face darkened. He took the rhodion and examined it more closely,

"Hmm... A rhodion transistor," he muttered, raising it to eye level. "We've been incorporating them into some of our fanciest orders for almost two years, even perfecting them as we've gone along. At each stage, we've handled about a dozen, between experimental settings, tests and measurements. We haven't kept a strict accounting of them, I'm afraid... Most of them ended up in the trash."

"Really?" Trump said, nonplussed. "Isn't your parent company afraid of leaks?"

"Why should they be? They already own several patents on this device. Besides, it hasn't been totally perfected yet. No competitor in the world would dare use it in their products without NOMO's consent. They would face a huge lawsuit."

"As long as NOMO finds out, of course," remarked Trump.

"We always do," said Ragusano. "In this area, especially, no new device can reach the market without a fraud of this type being immediately detected. I could tell you some stories..."

Trump thought about it, then concluded:

"So, any number of people could have slipped one of these into their pocket without being caught?"

"Well, yes, but I don't see how that's any of your business."

The turn of the conversation had changed Trump's theories. Yet, despite the plant manager's assurances, he could not believe that a spy like Zakuski had fumbled in trying to get a rhodion to his mysterious sponsor.

"Did your staff sign non-disclosure agreements?" he asked.

"For some specific products, yes, but not in general. Articles featuring our work are routinely published in several leading industry magazines."

"Including about the use of rhodion transistors?"

"Yes. Do I need to remind you that patents have been filed. Everyone knows about them. There's no secret there."

Trump remained dubious. Someone at the plant had, directly or through an intermediary, provided a rhodion to Zakuski, who had left the country with it—for no discernible purpose. Yet. But nothing proved that this scheme stopped there. Other items, more confidential ones, might have followed the same path. The leak was unquestionable. His Russian paymasters would want it to first be identified, then stopped.

Trump pulled out a letter that Stroganoff had sent him on Okhrana's letterhead, and showed it to Ragusano, who blanched. The pretense of installing cameras in a New York building was dropped.

"I want a list of all the technicians who've handled rhodions," Trump demanded. "Willingly or not, one of them was involved with a rival intelligence network."

Ragusano's bushy eyebrows shot up.

"That's a very serious charge, Mr. Trump."

"This rhodion was found in Zakuski's possession in Tijuana," Trump said, pointing at the item on the glass table. "The Okhrana would like to know how it got there, that's all."

"But it would have been legal for him to just mail it there…"

"Yes, but if he had shipped it out openly, I wouldn't be here. Unfortunately, the circumstances behind its transfer are quite suspicious. That's why I must insist."

Even though Ragusano wasn't Russian, he was working for a major Russian company, and the mention of the Okhrana had shaken him. Besides, if there was a black sheep working in his plant, he didn't want to protect him.

"Frankly, I have the utmost confidence in the morals of all our employees," he affirmed, "but it would be foolish of me to impede your investigation. At worst, I believe that you'll only discover that one of them may have been the victim of some kind of blackmail."

"I hope so," said Trump. "It happens more often than you think."

Ragusano took a sheet of paper and, from memory, started to write down the names and addresses of all the technicians working at the factory without changing his concerned expression.

As he wrote, Trump re-pocketed the rhodion transistor—a real electronic wonder with amazing properties. A sudden thought struck him.

"Other than Zakuski, have there been any other recent deaths in the company?"

Ragusano looked at him in surprise.

"No, thank God!" he replied.

"Good. Do you have anyone whose hobby might have something to do with the use of infrared equipment?"

After a short pause, Ragusano put down his pen.

"Is that a clue?" he asked Trump, blankly.

"No. Idle curiosity on my part. It's my hobby."

Reassured, the plant manager replied:

"We do have one. He was one of the first technicians I hired. His name is Ramon Bandel."

CHAPTER VIII

During the following days, Donald J. Trump re-mained mostly inactive, waiting for the report from the Russian agents watching Zakuski's condo.

He had also asked Stroganoff to conduct back-ground checks on all the technicians on Ragusano's list, but nothing unusual had turned up.

The Russians had placed a tap on Ramon Bandel's phone line, and that caught something that drew Trump's attention.

At first, the conversation between Bandel and a man named Henryk Lubelski seemed like entirely inno-cent banter between two friends, devoid of anything sus-picious. After the exchange of a few pleasantries, Lubelski had asked Bandel if he was going to the next party being held by a woman named Monique Saint-Albray.

He mentioned the names of several mutual friends who would definitely be going to the party. Her recent absence had temporarily interrupted the series of fun gatherings that took place at her home every week.

Bandel confirmed that he wouldn't dream of miss-ing the next party, and the conversation had then gone off in other directions.

Stroganoff's men had discovered that Lubelski was an electronics engineer working for a firm called Electronics Memories Magnetics located in Torrance.

Trump wondered who was this Mrs. Saint-Albray? And why was she giving parties for such highly specialized electronics engineers?

While the Okhrana agents gathered information about her, he decided to visit Lubelski at his home in Hermosa Beach.

He was greeted by a man in his forties, of medium height, with graying temples. Wearing glasses, the engineer had the gravity one expected to find in a dedicated scientist.

Trump introduced himself as a buyer of electronic components for one of his father's firms in New York and was led into a beige living room.

"I'm here in an unofficial capacity," he said in a soothing voice. "I was hoping for some details on Mrs. Saint-Albray's parties."

Lubelski looked nonplussed.

"There's nothing mysterious or compromising about them," he said with a hint of annoyance. "We're not a bunch of perverts."

Trump smiled.

"I wouldn't mind if you were; I'm a bit of a pervert myself," he said, smiling. "No, I'm not interested in that, but I need to find out a little more about these evenings to stop any fake gossip. In fact, I'm counting on your discretion, because I don't want to bother anyone else unnecessarily."

Lubelski indicated that Trump should sit, and also sat down in an armchair.

"What exactly do you want to know?" asked the engineer.

"Tell me who her most frequent guests are, what you think of Mrs. Saint-Albray, and so on. I'm not after any dirt, I just want to get an idea of the ambiance there, that's all."

Lubelski, feeling reassured, lifted his hands from the armrests.

"What can I tell you... The evenings are pretty friendly. Our small circle is quite open. Like everyone else, I appreciate the good humor and informality. We talk, we discuss, we exchange views in a relaxed atmosphere. Mrs. Saint-Albray is charming; she likes to bring together people with a variety of interests. Her style, elegance and sophistication are quite remarkable."

"Can you give me the names of some of the other guests?"

"Since you've found me, it shouldn't be difficult for you to find the others."

"That's true, but you could at least save me time if you told me the more prominent names."

Lubelski effortlessly rattled off those that came to him:

"There's Beaufort and Castello, two colleagues of mine from EMM; Derby, a research assistant at UCLA; Mizithra, from the USC Medical School; Dunbarra, a mathematician from the Lerner Institute; Bandel, from NOMO; Barkanit, a chemist who works for BSF; Roncal, from Hughes Aircraft... And others..."

Trump immediately realized that a gathering of elite scientists like that was bound to excite the greed of professional spies.

"Are there any women at these parties?" he asked, incidentally.

"Sometimes," Lubelski replied. "They are usually the companions or guests of one of the regulars. I remember a Janine Cantal, a friend of Mrs. Saint-Albray's, who worked for the Laroche Laboratories in France."

"Are there any foreigners present?"

"Occasionally. When a scientist of any renown is visiting Los Angeles, Mrs. Saint-Albray makes a point of inviting him."

"Is she a scientist herself, or just a snob who likes to surround herself with accomplished men?"

Lubelski weighed his answer.

"I think she enjoys the company of educated men, and she prefers scientists over the more ephemeral glory of movie stars and politicians. She's definitely intelligent, but I don't think she has a university degree."

"Is she married?"

"She was, but her husband died six years ago. I never met him, but I think he was some kind of oil man—the Stalco refineries, I believe. She's certainly very wealthy.

"Is she attractive?"

Lubelski coughed, and rubbed his cheek.

"She's a very pretty woman," he conceded with a faint trace of embarrassment. "Some of the guests flirt with her shamelessly; I suppose it's unavoidable... But I don't think she's ever encouraged anyone to go any further, and from what I've heard, her private life is irreproachable."

Trump couldn't help but be somewhat skeptical of that, but didn't let it show.

"I understand she was traveling recently. Do you know where she went?"

"Vegas, I think. She goes often. I think she owns some commercial properties there."

"When was the last party?"

"Two weeks ago."

"Do you remember what you talked about?

Lubelski looked confused.

"You know, we talk about a lot of things... We constantly jump from one subject to another. Little groups form, then break up... It's rare for everyone to listen to a single speaker..."

Trump tried to help.

"Did you discuss anything about electronics, for instance?"

"Let me see," Lubelski said thoughtfully. "The subject is pretty topical... because of the recent exploits of the French terrestrial and lunar satellite launches. Wait! It's coming back to me! Yes, we did! Bandel began with a speech on the crossover that could soon be achieved between millimeter wave radios and the upper part of the infrared spectrum, through the further development of rhodion transistors. After that, we started talking about passive radar, space exploration, and other areas of high-frequency applications that were, frankly, pretty out there! Fontina, who works at JPL, mentioned the upcoming arrival of a delegation of French rocket scientists, who've participated in the exciting work being done in Reganne. Mrs. Saint-Albray was interested and asked Rubin to invite them to her next party."

Trump, listening to Lubelski with great interest, absentmindedly lit a *Gitane*. He thought that the Russians would be smart to plant a mole in the attractive widow's circle of friends. Maybe the French already had...

"I suppose anything to do with space travel is hot right now," he admitted. "Did you ever have the feeling that your conversations were directed?"

"Directed? What do you mean?"

"Like maybe someone might have tried to use your chats as a clever way of finding out something that might have been a matter of national security?"

Lubelski stared at Trump, more amused than outraged.

"You're way off base there, Mr. Trump. We're not some kind of high-powered think tank discussing secret strategies, just a bunch engineers who like to hear themselves talk!"

"Well, even secret strategies have to start somewhere," said Trump, "and often, they start in laboratories, with new discoveries. All the great powers are always on the lookout for the next revolutionary breakthrough."

Lubelski made a dismissive gesture.

"That may well be," he said, "but all of us have agreed to leave the burning questions of the day at the door. We're a peaceful bunch, and the potential usage of our research by the military doesn't thrill us. Things like that are above our pay grade. Besides, we tend to ramble on, and rarely mention anything specific; we aren't exchanging formulas and equations."

Trump remained skeptical, but chose to appear reassured and satisfied.

"OK," he said, getting up. "Thanks for your help. You've convinced me that Mrs. Saint-Albray's parties are harmless. I'd appreciate it if you forgot we even had this conversation."

"I understand," Lubelski said, nodding, his patriotism obvious. "And if you have any more concerns, don't hesitate to contact me again."

"I honestly don't believe that will be necessary," replied Trump, convincingly.

CHAPTER IX

Two more days passed before Boris Stroganoff could share the reports he had assembled from his various teams with Donald J. Trump.

No one had visited Zakuski's condominium in Hollywood, except for Poshekhonsky, who had returned to cart away all the equipment in a rented van.

Poshekhonsky had then visited a few of Zakuski's clients to deliver the back orders. Finally, he had booked passage on a train to Mexico. An agent of the Okhrana had been ordered to follow him.

As for Mrs. Saint-Albray, she had been born Monique Boursin, in Fontainebleau, France, on 22 December 1939. Her parents had moved to Algeria, where she had lost them during the Troubles. She had ended up in a refugee camp, then emigrated to the United States, where she had acquired U.S. citizenship by marrying Joseph Saint-Albray, an oil refining magnate, who had died of a heart attack three years after their marriage, bequeathing her his entire fortune.

She had returned home from Las Vegas the day before, and was now kept under constant surveillance by the Okhrana. She lived in a mansion on Mulholland Drive in the Hollywood Hills, and she often traveled, both in the U.S. and abroad. She employed three servants: a chauffeur, a maid and a butler. Stroganoff's agents had failed to discover if she had a lover, as part of her busy social life.

In keeping with his plan, Trump returned to the condo in Hollywood.

Now that all the equipment that had filled the place was gone, it seemed larger. He noted that, on the balcony, the infrared "telescope" was still there.

Poshekhonsky had therefore considered it the personal property of the deceased, just the same as all the items of clothing that he had left behind.

Stroking his chin, Trump wandered around the workshop. A glance out of the window caused him to notice the "Hollywoodland" sign in the distance—and Mulholland Drive just below. Could Zakuski have used his infrared devices to communicate with Mrs. Saint-Albray?

Was it to point a finger at her that Colonel Roquefort had returned the rhodion transistor?

Trump regretted that the beautiful Mrs. Saint-Albray had returned home a day early. He would have liked to search her house in her absence.

He left the condo building and drove back to his office at the Sberbank Tower in Downtown Los Angeles.

Once there, he called Stroganoff.

"The telescope is still there," he reported, with a shadow of regret. "If he bought it here, that trail has gone cold."

"I'll check," said the Russian spymaster.

"I wiped it carefully, so it can still function as a trap. If someone touches it, they'll leave fingerprints. Let's check again in a few days."

"Do you really think someone could get in there without our agents catching them?"

"It's possible. Don't you find it suspicious that it wasn't removed right after Zakuski's death?"

"No, not particularly."

"I do. You don't leave behind a clue like that, unless you plan to use it again."

"Or maybe, you're too careful to fall into an obvious trap," retorted Stroganoff. "Both hypotheses have merit. Let me remind you that we haven't established as fact that Zakuski used that infrared device to receive messages... For all we know, he might have used it to take spectacular pictures of Hollywood at night or stare into women's bedrooms!"

"Yes," said Trump, ironic, "and he used the electric iron to fix the crease of his pants while waiting for the girls to undress."

Stroganoff let the issue drop and moved on to another topic:

"I'm afraid I have some bad news, Donald. Balkansky from the *Razvedupr*[2] has requested we reassign our agents in Los Angeles to a more pressing matter. I can't tell you what it's about, but it's a top priority. So this means no more men available to watch the condo, the NOMO factory or Mrs. Saint-Albray..."

"That's stupid! Why?" Trump rebelled. "We're just starting to..."

"Believe me, it's unavoidable," cut in Stroganoff. "In any event, I was going to tell you that Mrs. Saint-Albray has just booked a seat on the next *Silver Arrow* to Mexico. Just in case, I informed Kougloff, our man in Tijuana, whom I'd already assigned to tail Poshekhonsky."

Trump's eyebrows drew together.

---

[2] Russian military intelligence.

"She left already, right after she came back?"

"Yes. Call me suspicious, but do you know what else happened today? The delegation of French scientists who came to Pasadena was attacked."

"What?" Trump shouted. "Any deaths?"

"One. And three wounded, one seriously. A bomb exploded in the room where they were attending a banquet in their honor organized by the American Rocket Society and the French-American Chamber of Commerce and Industry. I've heard that the explosives were traced back to Mexico."

"This is bad... very bad," said Trump. "It's going to have a serious impact on Franco-Mexican relations. So that's why the *Razvedupr* asked you to put everyone on high alert?"

"Yes. Unless they arrest the culprits within the next twenty-four hours, there's going to be consequences," said Stroganoff. "And we might get caught in the crossfire. It's a foregone conclusion that someone will try to blame Russia. For such important figures to be the victims of such an aggression during their stay here in the United States is unprecedented. The conspiracy theorists will have a field day."

"Well, your guys know their stuff. At least, continue searching through the background of these people—especially Mrs. Saint-Albray—with a fine tooth comb."

"And what are you planning to do now?"

"Since she's flown the coop, I'm going to use her absence to try to find something worthwhile. Her strange parties and constant traveling strike me as damn suspicious..."

CHAPTER X

A Los Angeles Department of Water and Power repairman appeared the next morning at Mrs. Saint-Albray's mansion in the Hollywood Hills. The butler who opened the door was told that the visitor was there to check the wires due to abnormalities that had been detected in the area.

His equipment, his DWP uniform and ID, and his serious attitude convinced the manservant of the authenticity of his visit.

In fact, he was Frank Capra (no relation), an employee of the Los Angeles branch of the Trump Organization, and Donald J. Trump often used him for undercover jobs.

After showing the fake DWP technician the electric meter, the butler asked him how long the work would take.

"An hour or two," replied Capra. "I have to test every circuit breaker in every room of the house."

Knowing that his employer was away, the butler had no real desire to spend the rest of the morning with the DWP repairman.

"Make yourself at home," he said. "When you're done, come find me in the kitchen."

"Sure will," said Capra jovial, unpacking his equipment. "I ain't afraid of the dark!"

After a few perfunctory checks, Capra went to see if Mrs. Saint-Albray, in addition to her collection of valuable Persian rugs and *objets d'art*, didn't also have microphones connected to a tape recorder inside her house.

The various rooms and salons were explored with more meticulous care than most genuine DWP employees would have displayed, but Capra found nothing unusual, except that her electrical wiring really did need to be upgraded.

The butler came back twice, inquiring if everything was in order. The second time, Capra expressed serious reservations about the condition of the wiring, and told him he had found quite a few things that were not up to code. He asked to talk to the owner.

"She isn't here right now," said the manservant. "She hasn't told me when she'll be back. She never does..."

"That's a shame," complained Capra. "It means I'll have to come back. I still have to check the circuits on the second floor and in the attic. Will you show me the way?"

The butler led him to the top floor, walked around with him, and pointed out the use of the various rooms, before concluding:

"I'll leave you be. I'm still not finished in the kitchen."

Despite the freedom granted to him, Capra couldn't carry out a complete search of Mrs. Saint-Albray's mansion. There were too many rooms, too much furniture, too many knickknacks. Nevertheless, he successively checked a library, a home office, and a master bedroom with *en suite* bathroom. There, he paused before a fine art photograph of a stunningly beautiful woman inserted in a tasteful silver frame—it was a portrait of the mistress of the house when she was younger. With her blond hair, refined features, and seductive grey eyes, Monique Saint-Albray, a millionaire widow, must attract a lot of suitors, he thought.

Having reached the top of the house, Capra went inside a large linen closet lit by a window overlooking the back of the property, through which he could see the Hollywoodland sign in the distance.

Next to a white painted closet, an ironing board supported an electric iron placed upright on its end.

Capra listened. A vacuum cleaner was running on the floor below.

The closet was locked. Capra opened his bag again, taking out an instrument that was not part of the DWP's standard equipment and quickly began to pick the lock. It didn't take long.

Both doors opened with a small squeak. Folded sheets were piled on the shelves. Tablecloths and pillowcases were stored on racks. But the highest shelf seemed empty.

Capra climbed onto a chair, and saw a long wooden box pushed against the rear of the closet. He pulled it out and opened it.

Inside was an enameled tube, twenty-five inches long, both ends covered with black plastic caps, resting on tissue paper. An electric cord was wrapped around it and the components of a telescopic tripod were stored in a parallel compartment.

Jubilant, Capra hastened to put everything back in place. Trump had been right. The circle was closed. Monique Saint-Albray, who had repeatedly entertained

Ramon Bandel at her parties, was in secret communication with Pavel Zakuski!

To avoid attracting suspicion, Capra lingered on the floor for an extra half hour. Then he calmly went downstairs, found the butler in the kitchen and asked him to sign an authentic-looking, dirty DWP visit report book, before leaving the mansion.

"I was totally right," crowed Donald J. Trump when he called Stroganoff later. "The lovely Mrs. Saint-Albray owns the same equipment as our late friend, Mr. Zakuski. They could send each other infrared signals at any time of day or night, even in bad weather, across the rooftops of Hollywood."

Stroganoff sucked on his cigarette-holder.

"This is now a fact, yes," he admitted. "If these two were connected, it is almost certain that other information or devices using the same channel have been illegally taken abroad, and the rhodion transistor may well be but a small example of what has been pilfered."

"Mrs. Saint-Albray's home is a nexus of invaluable information," said Trump. "I think that broad doesn't like to get her hands dirty: she limits herself to sharing information that others exploit, if they feel like it. Until Zakuski is replaced, we don't have a chance of catching or disabling her network. I bet he was the backbone of her organization.

Trump paused for a second, then added:

"In a way, I find it worrying that she's gone to Mexico. Could she have gotten scared after learning of his death?"

"She travels a lot," said Stroganoff. "Her sudden departure does not necessarily imply that she's taken flight. Anyway, I think she went there for a reason: either she felt threatened in Los Angeles, or she went to see someone."

"We shouldn't give her an inch of leeway, or she'll slip through our fingers. As much as I hate it to do it, and despise Mexico, considering that you're short-handed right now, I may have to follow her."

"Yes," Stroganoff agreed. "Personally, I would prefer it if she came back, not only so we can discover the ins and outs of her network, but also so we can use her and her parties as a way to spread disinformation. Can you imagine the fake news that we could propagate through her?"

A knowing smile crossed Trump's lips.

"The fact is, it would be hard to find a better medium for a disinformation campaign," he agreed. "But we need to know who's pulling her strings."

After a moment of reflection, Stroganoff decided:

"Go to Tijuana and find out what Mrs. Saint-Albray is doing there, Donald. Follow her wherever she goes. If it looks like she plans to stay there, we might have to take more drastic steps like taking her prisoner. Kougloff will assist you."

CHAPTER XI

The next day, Donald J. Trump got off the *Silver Arrow* bullet train at Tijuana's Garcia station. He took a taxi to the Gran Hotel Imperial on Paseo Playas where he had reserved a suite.

The drive there revealed to him how much the city had changed in the six years since he last had visited it, looking for a suitable location for a hotel. Entire neighborhoods had grown over once rural areas and huge buildings now stood in its downtown area. The people appeared to be better dressed, and there were many more cars. Despite a few poor areas, one felt that Tijuana had shed its colonial past and embraced the new regime's prosperity.

Fifteen minutes later, Trump was checking in at the hotel, where Kougloff was already waiting for him.

Soon the two men were sitting in a brightly decorated suite with view over the Pacific Ocean.

While only slightly smaller than Trump, Kougloff was so unremarkable physically that he would have challenged the ability of a policeman tasked with writing down his description. He was neither fat nor thin, with no special features, and had tired, brown eyes devoid of any personality: dead eyes. Nothing in him betrayed any wit or courage, even though he knew how to rise to the occasion if needed. His clothes were as unremarkable as his face.

Kougloff asked the first question:

"So, what do we have on Mrs. Saint-Albray?"

"French by birth, she married a wealthy Californian oil refiner, who had the good sense to kick the bucket soon afterwards, leaving her a vast fortune. On the surface, there's nothing suspicious about his death, but it does make you wonder. Since then, she's turned to espionage, although again, we don't have any real evidence of wrongdoing. Not enough to turn her in to the FBI, anyway. What's she been doing since she arrived?"

Kougloff pulled out a small notebook, his face as expressive as if he had just been told the time of day.

"She's booked a suite at the local downtown Hilton, which is quite close to the French Embassy, although that might be a coincidence," he uttered in a monotone voice. "I managed to book a suite close to hers. I'm afraid Stroganoff is going to have a heart attack when he sees the bill. Is this operation going to take a long time?"

"No idea," replied Trump, spreading his hands. "We've got to find out what she's doing here."

"Shopping, so far. Lots of it. Each time she goes out, she returns with a ton of bags. Otherwise, she takes walks and, to all appearances, she hasn't met anyone."

"She made no attempt to lose you?"

Kougloff shook his head no.

"I don't think she even spotted me."

"No attempts to contact any French or Mexican handler?"

"None whatsoever. She's behaving like an ordinary tourist."

"I assume you've found a way to tap her phone and check her mail?"

"That's a problem. I'm afraid I couldn't," admitted Kougloff. "The Hilton has direct dial-out facilities, and I haven't been able to plant a bug directly in her room. So I don't know who she may have been talking to, or even meeting. I can't very well park myself on her doorstep."

"Maybe you could sleep in her bed?" sneered Trump.

Kougloff ignored the joke, instead contemplating it as a viable option.

"You'd be better suited to that than I," he replied with imperturbable gravity.

"I should grab her by the pussy," said Trump, "but I think she has too much class."

"I think so too."

Trump changed the subject:

"What's the political climate like in Mexico right now?"

Kougloff grimaced.

"Since the Mexican Empire claimed its independence from the French, the tension between Russia and Mexico has decreased, but it's become a no man's land and free for all for spies of all nationalities. Also, as the drug trafficking has gone up, so has the power of the local cartels. You'll need a gun. I've arranged for it. Also, I've pulled two of our best men from the station in Durango: Rossiysky and Kostromskoy. You'll meet them later. Do you plan to assist us in the surveillance of Mrs. Saint-Albray?"

"I have to. I should move to the Hilton."

"As soon as you've got a suite there, I'll have my men report to you."

"I'm only interested if she makes contact with someone who's a valuable target."

"I understand. I'm also going to give you a local phone number you can call day or night if you need assistance. Simply say 'Cheese' to the operator."

"It's like being in an enemy country," smiled Trump.

"Don't joke about this. No day goes by here without a shooting or kidnapping, or both. Don't be fooled by the peaceful, carefree atmosphere. We don't want you to end up in a Tijuana tango, like Zakuski."

"Tijuana tango?"

"Dancing with a car. It's one of the ways they get rid of people here when they don't want any trouble. They knock them out, then run them over with their car. The police usually report it as an accident, but they know better."

Trump reflected, then said:

"That's exactly what I'm afraid of: that our friend Mrs. Saint-Albray suddenly evaporates without a trace. This city is the perfect place to disappear. Willingly or not."

"*Da!* You've got to have lived here to know how necessary it is to watch where you're putting your feet before you go out."

CHAPTER XII

That same evening, Donald J. Trump moved into the Hilton. Brightly lit, the hotel was a symbol of American opulence.

Indeed, it was mostly filled by Americans who spoke little or no Spanish or French, and one could hear more English being spoken in the lobby than either of them.

Trump was assigned a suite on the sixteenth floor, the floor just below Mrs. Saint-Albray. When he stepped into the room, he could almost believe that he was still in the United States, until he glanced out of the window and saw the view below. Spread before him was the slick but relatively empty downtown business district, and beyond that a cluster of rundown houses. To the left stood a few rectangular high-rises, separated by large patches of nothing.

This vision contradicted the impression that he had had in the taxi earlier; despite some recent business developments, Tijuana remained what it had always been.

Trump ordered a copious a meal—American food—and ate in his room.

Whatever her tastes, Mrs. Saint-Albray had not come here simply to shop. It was far more likely that her multiple visits to upscale boutiques were purely designed to mislead any followers... As Kougloff had pointed out, she could have easily discussed her goals with anyone on the telephone without the Okhrana agents being the wiser.

After dinner, Trump watched American television direct from KFMB San Diego, called Kougloff for a status update, and went to bed.

The next morning, while Trump was finishing his breakfast, there was a knock at the door.

"Mrng," mumbled Trump, his mouth full, as he opened the door.

A bare-headed man in a suit entered the room. Less than thirty years-old, he still looked like a schoolboy. He closed the door behind him, and said in a respectful tone:

"I'm Rossiysky. Kougloff must have told you about me."

"Yes. He was going to introduce us later today. Sit. You want a cup of coffee?"

"No, thank you," the Russian said, accepting the seat that his host had pointed out to him.

"Why the long face?" asked Trump.

"I think we have a problem, *gospodin*."

"What's wrong? Is it Mrs. Saint-Albray?"

"No, it's worse than that," said the visitor in a low voice, as if he were afraid that microphones were hidden in the walls. "She left the hotel last night and Kostromskoy was shadowing her. Then she returned here—I am sure of that, because I was sitting in the lobby and I saw her, but my colleague has given no sign of life since."

Trump's brow furrowed.

"When was he supposed to switch with you?"

"As soon as he returned. Worst case, this morning at 7 if he had had a serious reason to be away overnight."

There was silence in the room.

"And you're sure he hasn't come back?" Trump asked, concerned.

"Absolutely sure," Rossiysky said. "I even called her suite to check if she was still there…"

As Trump raised an eyebrow, he hastened to add:

"I asked for *la señora* Cotija, and she thought it was a mistake of the switchboard.

Trump stared ahead.

"What kind of guy is Kostromskoy? Is he a team player, or a lone wolf?"

"No worries there! He's totally reliable! He was in the top ten at the Institute."[3]

"Have you told Kougloff?"

"Yes, of course! I saw him just before I came here. He has not given another mission to Kostromskoy, nor has he received any call from him."

Trump finished his plate in silence, drank the rest of his coffee, wiped his lips with a napkin, and lit a *Gitane*.

"It's clear you were made," he concluded. "She's been wandering around for two days so someone else could check if she was being followed. And when she needed to be alone, they just 'disappeared' the guy who was following her."

Rossiysky vigorously scratched his reddish-blond hair.

"What you say is probably true, *gospodin*," he reluctantly admitted. "But who would have imagined that this pretty girl was dragging her own bodyguards around with her?"

---

[3] Russian spy school.

"Something to never forget," Trump said, conveniently omitting the numerous times he had committed the same mistake

. "In short, you're toast, buddy, and the best thing for you to do now is to stay quietly in your room."

"But what about Kostromskoy!" protested Rossiysky, his face reddening. Are we just going to drop it and forget him?"

"Of course not. But we need a different strategy."

"Like what? I see only one way: to kidnap the bitch and make her talk."

"Maybe, but that should be our final option. What does she know? Is she even aware of what happened? We're not sure of anything."

Disappointed, Rossiysky got up and asked:

"And in the meantime, what? To continue tailing her is to run the risk of me disappearing too? If you don't want to kidnap and question her, what's left?"

Trump, tapping with his index finger on his cigarette to get the ashes to drop in the ashtray, replied:

"If she tries to leave Tijuana, we'll grab her. But as long as she stays here, I want to catch the goons protecting her."

CHAPTER XIII

Mrs. Saint-Albray left the Hilton at six thirty that evening. Her clothes were less elegant than usual. She wore a tweed travel coat, flat-heeled shoes and her bouffant hairdo was concealed by a scarf tied under her chin.

She took the Avenida Juan Nepomuceno Almonte and quietly walked towards the church of El Espiritu Santo, which stood proudly as one of the new shrines to Catholic worship erected during the Imperial Government's campaign for the restoration of faith.

Rossiysky followed her closely, almost openly. His coat collar turned up, both hands in his pockets, he walked, keeping his head down. A fine mist was falling from a sky the color of soot.

Donald J. Trump left his observation post after Rossiysky had gone about a hundred yards, after carefully monitoring the movements of both passersby and traffic on the Avenida, hoping to catch any spotters.

Arriving near the church, Mrs. Saint-Albray walked around it, then, leaving the large avenue with its well-lit shops, cinemas and restaurants, she veered towards the closest metro station, José Mariano de Salas.

While striving to see if anyone among the throng of pedestrians was paying particular attention to Rossiysky, Trump also made sure that there were no vehicles traveling at slow speed tailing him. When he realized that Mrs. Saint-Albray and the Russian agent were going into the subway, he accelerated his pace so he wouldn't fall too far behind them.

The dense crowd in the station allowed Trump to slip between groups of travelers without attracting anyone's attention. In any event, he hoped that any eventual enemy agents were keeping their eyes on Rossiysky, and not the dozens of anonymous travelers who were preparing to board one of the trains.

Trump lost time buying a ticket, and stepped on the platform just as a train was coming out of the tunnel. He chose to ride in the last car, while Mrs. Saint-Albray and Rossiysky stood in the one located in the middle of the train.

The doors closed and the train left the station. With signs indicating the sequence of stations and the terminus of the line, Trump realized that the train was going to Rosarito.

Standing near one of the doors, in the direction of travel, he could see people entering and leaving the cars at every station.

After a while, the train emerged from below ground and continued its journey on the surface. Station followed station, monotonously, and at each stop more people got on and off, men, women and children jostled towards available seats and exits.

After La Joya, Trump's vigilance redoubled.

It had been agreed that morning that Rossiysky would not continue to act as bait beyond that point and would stop following their target. He had to abandon his journey, even if she continued hers.

When the train stopped at Campestre La Gloria, where one could change trains and take another line to Real Del Mar, Rossiysky got off.

Trump bent slightly to look through the window. His height facilitated things. Above the heads of the people who passed in front of him moving on the platform, he spotted Rossiysky walking towards the correspondence.

Whether the Okhrana agent was being followed or not was impossible to determine because of the flood of travelers.

Trump hesitated for a few seconds before the automatic doors closed. His decision to stay on the train was made in the hope that, if Mrs. Saint-Albray was protected by discreet bodyguards, they would have been concerned about Rossiysky, not himself.

The train was no longer as crowded. Trump mentally reviewed the precautions he had taken with Kougloff in case he was forced to venture further into Mexico.

At Lucio Blanco, a new batch of arrivals again filled the cars, which had been almost empty. Mrs. Saint-Albray remained in her seat.

The train finally arrived at Rosarito, the end of the line. Trump got off and easily spotted Mrs. Saint-Albray's grey tweed coat amongst the crowd milling on the platform, walking towards the exit.

There were mostly men interposed between him and his target. Following them, he climbed the stairs, and emerged into a poorly lit area, a crossroads where three rather large avenues intersected, with a few shops and houses.

Once most of the people has gone in various directions, Trump was overwhelmed by a feeling of loneliness. This dreary suburb, with its scant traffic, seemed strangely silent and deserted.

Mrs. Saint-Albray walked ahead, without appearing concerned about her surroundings, as if the place was familiar to her. While pretending to consult the metro map displayed at the exit of the station, Trump watched her silhouette shrinking in the distance.

Now convinced that nobody was watching her back, and that, in that respect, his plan had failed, Trump decided to clarify the reasons for this wealthy Angeleno widow to visit such a suburb at night.

He set off with long strides to catch up with her. Here and there, light shone from the windows, but there were large vacant lots covered with weeds and car wrecks between the blocks of buildings.

Mrs. Saint-Albray suddenly stopped in front of a two-story house. Trump had just enough time to jump behind a corner when she looked around as she waited for a response to her ring.

She disappeared inside the building, the pavement fleetingly lit by the light from inside the house when the door was opened.

Trump waited for several minutes, then left his improvised refuge. Passing in front of the house, he noticed that the ground floor was occupied by a store selling cameras and Kodak film, judging from the advertising painted on the front.

He continued walking straight ahead, looking for a place where he could hide, so as to not wander aimlessly through the lifeless neighborhood.

That Mrs. Saint-Albray might be affiliated with the *Dirección Imperial de Seguridad*, or DIS, the intelligence service of the Second Empire of Mexico was a perfectly probable working hypothesis. Its leaders were trying by all means possible to improve their own prestige with the French, and their own DIS could provide them with many advantages.

But why would the French, presumably aware of this, wish to throw a spanner in the works? And without being too obvious about it? The attitude of Colonel Roquefort seemed to indicate that direction...

Trump saw an abandoned house in need of major restoration and decided to stand watch in its entrance between the support beams. All he had to do was watch to see the door of the building where Mrs. Saint-Albray was.

And was Kostromskoy there too?

This was now a more risky business. Who knew if the missing Okhrana agent wasn't rotting in a DIS cell in Mexicali? Or worse…

Taking Mrs. Saint-Albray prisoner and keeping her as a hostage to trade against the Russian was a possible solution, now that they knew of this place and could launch a further investigation later.

Everything depended on whether the woman returned to the Hilton or not. Trump, alone, could not mount a permanent vigil. He planned to return to the train station in time to catch the last metro, and share what he'd learned with Kougloff.

He glanced at both sides of the street, and suddenly saw two men come out of the camera shop. Lit briefly, they walked to the other end of the street, and turned the corner.

Trump didn't move. Mrs. Saint-Albray remained his primary target. But the departure of these two individuals, who were certainly not customers, since the store was closed, made him wonder if a meeting hadn't taken place inside.

He waited for other signs of activity, while regretting being too far away to see the details of the figures leaving. Another twenty minutes passed without anyone else coming out of the shop.

When the door finally did open again, it was for Mrs. Saint-Albray to leave.

She walked back in the direction from which she had come, towards the metro station.

Trump was relieved to see her and not be forced to hang around the dilapidated house for another hour. He followed her. Seeing nothing to tell him the name of the street, he tried to burn any details capable of later pinpointing the location into his memory.

He also retraced his steps to the station, Mrs. Saint-Albray preceding him by a hundred yards. She reached the station and entered, running down the flight of steps, hurrying to catch the last train.

Trump accelerated his pace and crossed the square.

Suddenly, two dark shapes emerged from behind the metro map and approached him.

"*Dirección Imperial de Seguridad. Papeles, por favor,*" uttered one of the individuals in a menacing tone.

CHAPTER XIV

Donald J. Trump was sorely tempted, irrationally, to hook the man's leg and send him tumbling down the stairs.

But he immediately realized the stupidity of such an act, especially since he was a legitimate American businessman and had all the necessary papers to prove it.

So, without protesting, he handed his passport to the plainclothes officer. Dressed in black raincoats, hatless, the two Mexican agents looked at him suspiciously.

While one of them examined his papers, the other just stood there, hands in his pockets, attentive and scowling.

The first man pocketed Trump's passport and ordered in a harsh, accented voice:

"Come with us."

The second moved his right hand and the rough shape of a gun pointed at Trump appeared inside his pocket.

The notion that he might have been entrapped crossed Trump's mind, but he rejected it on the spot. No one had known ahead of time what his intentions had been. He also considered his chances if he started a brawl, but decided that, for the time being, they weren't good.

Instead, he replied in an indifferent voice:

"*Con gusto.*"

The two agents led him to a black car parked behind the train station.

Trump was unceremoniously pushed onto the back seat, where he was joined by one of the men. The other got behind the wheel and drove off.

Not a word had been exchanged.

Suspecting that he would soon be subjected to questioning, Trump prepared his answers, since stammering and delivering false statements about his supposed reasons for being here would only land him in more trouble. Fortunately, his cover was airtight, because he did intend to build a hotel-casino in Tijuana at some point in the future.

The car rolled northeast. After a long drive through the desolate suburbs of Camino Verde, it finally stopped in front of a hovel, which certainly didn't look like a police station or an official building. It might have been a restaurant once, but certainly no food had been served there for a long time.

They got out of the car. It was pitch black; the car's headlights provided the only source of light.

Feeling that he was about to enter the lair of a gang of cutthroats, Trump's plan changed. He stomped on the foot of one of his guards, shoved him with his shoulder while grabbing the sleeve of the other. The first man fell, head first, and hit his forehead against the car. The second tried to draw his weapon, but in vain. His hand clutched the gun in his pocket, but he was unable to pull it out.

Before he had time to use his left arm, Trump hit him in the hollow of the cheek. The violence of the shock caused the man to stumble, mouth agape.

Trump grabbed his arm, and twisted him to relieve him of his automatic. His opponent was clever enough to not resist, bowing with his body, and when Trump, now in possession of the gun, was holding him with only one hand, he freed himself abruptly. His fingers then closed like a vise on the American's forearm, preventing him from shooting.

Instead of trying to raise the automatic, Trump lowered his arm and hit his opponent in the stomach with his knee. The Mexican let go of his grip and dropped to the ground. Trump used that opportunity to kick him in the gut.

Leaping into the car, Trump tried to restart it, but the other man—the driver—had removed the key.

As he got out, the man who had hit his head against the trunk of the car, and had now recovered, jumped him from behind, having used the open door to hide his presence. Because of his bone spurs, Trump could not turn around in time. A fierce blow landed on his skull. He instinctively clung to the door, but his legs faltered. He was hit a second time by the butt of a gun, knocking him out for good.

He dropped to the ground, his elbow on the floor of the car.

"*Hurra!*" crowed his attacker. "Alfredo! I got him!"

The other man, his features still clenched with pain, joined his partner, holding his stomach. He threw a venomous look at Trump's slumped body, then muttered in Spanish:

"Can you drag him inside by yourself, Manuel? I don't think I can help you.

Manuel was hardly in great shape either. His head was buzzing. Nevertheless, he had the presence of mind to give his gun to Alfredo. Then he grabbed the injured

Trump by the collar and pulled him flat to the ground. After closing the car, he handcuffed his victim before dragging him toward the house.

Breathing hard, Manuel managed to pull the large, inert mass inside. Alfredo lent him a hand after all. They crossed a corridor and went down to the basement with their burden, using a flashlight to see where they were going.

They dragged Trump into a sparsely furnished cellar that contained a wobbly table, three stools, an old wardrobe and a spirit stove set on a crate. Manuel lit an acetylene lamp that spread a greenish light throughout the room, highlighting its sordidness.

"Should I go and fetch Requesón, or do you want to do it?" he asked Alfredo.

"Go," grumbled the other, "but bring back some tequila."

He sat down on a wooden crate, rubbing his stomach and continuing to glare at the unconscious Trump with smoldering looks of hatred.

Manuel climbed the steps heavily. Alfredo heard the sound of the car driving away, then nothing. A heavy silence once again reigned inside the house.

He looked at his watch: it was a few minutes past 1 a.m. To kill time, while waiting for Manuel's return, he lit a cigarette and searched the pockets of the prisoner. He discovered the usual everyday's objects plus a billfold full of dollars, which he took.

Then, using the tap, he wet his handkerchief and dabbed it on Trump's face with the intention of reviving him.

CHAPTER XV

Donald J. Trump was just beginning to regain consciousness when the car returned.

Lying on the tiled floor, he waited patiently for the arrival of two individuals, one being Manuel, the other still unknown to him.

The newcomer looked at him thoughtfully, then said to Alfredo:

"Sit him up. I want to talk to him."

The two Mexicans lifted Trump roughly, placing him on a stool, his back to the wall and went to stand on either side of him.

The more Trump thought about it, the more he became convinced that these men were not genuine members of the DIS.

"Cards on the table, it's in your interest," declared Requesón with bonhomie. "Are you an agent of the CIA?"

Trump chose to remain silent, not yet having decided which cover story he should use. Lying came easily to him; it was a second nature.

"Don't be stupid," advised the Mexican. "We know how to interrogate people like you, and even you know that human strength has its limits. You weren't following la Señora Saint-Albray to flirt with her... No more than your colleague was, yesterday. Which service do you work for?"

Trump couldn't stand even the thought of physical pain. His experience—and in this case, his instructions—told him it was better to start a conversation rather than to remain completely silent. Besides, it was easier to tell a fancy tale when one was in possession of his full faculties rather than after a severe beating.

"I'm Donald J. Trump," he began. "I'm an American businessman. Who are you? Are you professional kidnappers? Are you planning to ask for ransom?"

Requesón shrugged.

"Come on, don't try to bluff. We've had our eyes on you from the moment you checked in at the Hilton. We saw you hide in that old abandoned house waiting for Monique. In fact, we were hoping an American agent would show up. We made arrangements for someone like you..."

Had Kostromskoy sold his captors on the idea that he was CIA instead of a Russian agent? That might explain their attitude.

Trump revised his previous supposition and deduced from the circumstances of his capture and the place where he was kept that his interlocutors had nothing to do with the Mexican DIS but instead belonged to some kind of illegal network.

"Suppose that I were CIA, responsible for checking what some of our citizens do when they go abroad," he declared in a bored tone. "Why do you care?"

Requesón smiled sardonically.

"We don't," he asserted. "It wouldn't bother us at all, but we'd like to find out who killed Pavel Zakuski..."

Trump raised his eyebrows.

"Pavel Zakuski? Who's he?"

He was such a good liar that his obvious good faith would have convinced even the most suspicious investigator, but somehow, Requesón wasn't sold.

"I'm not a fool," he said in a tone of reproach. "You Yankees only became interested in Monique's business after Zakuski's death. What did he reveal before he was killed?"

Had the NOMO representative been tortured by the French? Or the Mexicans? Trump felt he was now on very shaky ground.

"I'm really sorry," he said firmly, "but I never heard the name of Pavel Zakuski."

Phrasing it this way, he was sure not to contradict Kostromskoy who had never heard of Zakuski because Kougloff had never mentioned his name to him.

Trump's categorical tone and well-faked sincerity puzzled Requesón and his two associates. They were persuaded they were dealing with some kind of American spy, half-ally, half-enemy.

Requesón continued:

"Frankly, you'd better tell us who you're working for. Your being dead or alive doesn't matter to us. But it makes quite a difference to you, right?

"A huge one," admitted Trump. "But why would I lie if I worked for the CIA?"

The advantage of this lie was that it was practically impossible for Requesón to check it, while being consistent with the operation of which Mrs. Saint-Albray had been the target.

Now it was Requesón's turn to waver. He wasn't at all certain about the veracity of their prisoner's answers. There would have been nothing surprising in the Americans wanting to keep an eye on Mrs. Saint-Albray because of her travels and various activities, with or without connecting her to the allegedly accidental death of Pavel Zakuski.

Besides, even if they were, a mere "correspondent" like Trump wouldn't necessarily have been informed of Zakuski's existence.

"What were you asked to find out about Mrs. Saint-Albray?" asked Requesón.

"Simply to see if she had any connections with the French or the Russians," claimed Trump.

Meanwhile, Alfredo, his face hardening, had listened with visible impatience to the conversation between their leader and Trump. He only needed Requesón's word and he'd be more than delighted to beat up the American. In fact, he was looking forward to it.

But Requesón seemed to be losing interest in their prisoner, and asked him:

"Did you check his ID?"

"Yes," Alfredo growled, showing off Trump's passport. "It looks authentic."

Requesón examined it for a minute.

"I've read about him. He's an East Coast developer. A crook. Just the kind of stooge the CIA might use for a job like this. I still have some contacts on the other side of the border. I'm going to ask them to check him out. Meanwhile, you keep him on ice."

The two Mexicans grabbed Trump and pushed him out of the cellar. Their torch lit up a tunnel to the left of the stairs, leading to a smaller cellar, with dirt floor and stone walls, totally empty. They threw Trump inside. An iron door, with heavy bolts and a small rectangular spy hole, reflected the lamplight.

Alfredo pulled the door towards him, slammed it shut, then locked it by sliding the two iron bars into place.

A wave of cold air swept Trump's face. The ground was wet, with a puddle of water by the door. He was plunged into opaque darkness and heard no sounds. Unable to see, he got up and stepped forward, raising his hands. His fingers touched a slimy wall.

After an all too short exploration, he discovered that th miserable cell contained neither a seat, nor a pallet.

He was alone in the dark.

CHAPTER XVI

Monique Saint-Albray returned to the Hilton Hotel just after midnight. There were an unusual number of people milling about the reception area. A group of American tourists had just arrived and were checking in.

Mrs. Saint-Albray passed behind them discreetly and rushed into one of the elevators.

Rossiysky, who was sitting behind a plant in the bar, pretending to read, spotted her at once. He was eager to see Trump and find out what he had learned.

But his anxiety grew as time passed and Trump did not return. After twenty minutes, he decided to go back to his room.

He ordered a whiskey from room service and waited.

He dialed Trump's suite every half-hour, but there was never a response.

The plan was for Trump to follow Mrs. Saint-Albray back to the hotel. If Kostromskoy hadn't disappeared in the same way, Rossiysky wouldn't have been as concerned. But this was no coincidence.

Torn between the fear of appearing cowardly and that of acting too late, he decided to wait until 8 a.m. Until then, he consumed great quantities of alcohol and smoked cigarette after cigarette.

As the fateful deadline approached, Rossiysky put on his overcoat and headed downstairs.

In the reception area, the agitation had subsided. He walked quickly to the exit, and got into a taxi.

He changed cabs twice and, twenty minutes later, arrived at Kougloff's residence in Los Saucillos.

His boss immediately noticed that something was wrong. They hadn't even sat down before he asked:

"What's going on?"

A dismayed Rossiysky explained, adding:

"When I changed trains at Campestre La Gloria, I thought he was going to keep covering me. But he must have changed his mind when he noticed that there was nobody behind me. Since Mrs. Saint-Albray remained in the train, I think he decided to continue following her. But she's back at the hotel and he isn't. I thought you should know right away."

As stone-faced as usual, Kougloff cleared his throat.

"Well, Trump is usually careful," he emphasized. "I doubt he walked into a trap. You did well to come and see me, of course, but I think it's still too early to be alarmed. Maybe he found a trail leading to Kostromskoy; he would have wanted to follow it."

Despite his confidence in Kougloff, Rossiysky expressed skepticism.

"There are a thousand reasons why he may have stayed behind, but if you want my honest opinion, it's not his style to throw himself into the lion's den."

"But it's not impossible. If she was met by her contact when she left the metro, Trump might have followed them… Don't lose sight of the fact that his purpose was precisely to identify her contacts."

Sullenly, Rossiysky agreed:

"Yes, of course... Maybe I'm overreacting. But how long do we wait until we start to really worry?"

"Let's wait until tomorrow morning, Say, 7 a.m., an hour after the metro starts up again."

Seeing the disappointment on the face of the younger officer, Kougloff added:

"But this does not mean I'm going to sit here doing nothing. I'll report to Stroganoff and make some inquiries with the local police. Go back to the Hilton and wait there. Call me at 7 a.m. on the dot if Trump hasn't shown up. Then, I'll know that your fears were justified, and we'll act."

CHAPTER XVII

The next morning, Donald J. Trump was still missing, and, acting in accordance with Stroganoff's instructions, Kougloff launched Plan B.

Mrs. Saint-Albray left the hotel at 11 a.m., planning to do some shopping, then have lunch in one of Avenida Habsburg's stylish *cafés*. As she turned the corner from the hotel, she was approached by Kougloff and Rossiysky.

"FBI, Ma'm, please follow us," said the older man in a perfect American accent.

Mrs. Saint-Albray's composure faltered briefly; then, she reasserted herself.

"What?" she said, haughtily. "How dare you stop me, here... in a foreign city?"

"We have a rogatory commission. Our authority vis-à-vis US citizens is recognized by the local police," replied Kougloff. "Follow us without making a fuss, otherwise we will be obliged to use force."

At Kougloff's side, Rossiysky stared at her aggressively, looking more convincing than his somewhat sluggish boss.

Outraged, but guessing that open opposition would be useless, Mrs. Saint-Albray patted her hair coquettishly and protested:

"I don't understand what you want? If you want to see my passport, I'll show it to you. Everything is in perfect order."

She tried to open her purse, but Kougloff stopped her by putting his hand on her sleeve:

"Don't bother, Mrs. Saint-Albray," he said. "We'll see to that later. Are you coming voluntarily, or do we have to use force?"

She shrugged with irritation, kept her chin up and her eyes distant, but nevertheless walked in the direction Kougloff had indicated, that is to say along the crosswalk leading to the 10 de Abril park.

While staying very close to her, Rossiysky cast a quick glance over his shoulder to check if anyone was following them, or even paying them close attention.

The trio crossed the park and approached a black Citroën Traction Avant with a California license plate. Kougloff opened the back door.

"Get in," he ordered Mrs. Saint-Albray.

Her face hostile, she bent down and slid into the back seat. Rossiysky settled next to her, and slammed the door.

Kougloff sat in the driver's seat and started the engine.

As soon as the car was in motion, Rossiysky half turned his head to look out through the rear window. The car skirted the zoo, followed the roundabout at Marron, then began to travel towards the US border.

"What is the point of this?" Mrs. Saint-Albray asked Rossiysky, who, being younger, she felt, might be more compliant. "Why is the FBI interested in me?"

Rossiysky, despite being slightly attracted to her beauty and fragrance, responded curtly.

"You'll know soon. And don't try anything; it'd be a waste of time,"

Mrs. Saint-Albray shrugged.

"Can I at least smoke?"

"I'd rather you use one of mine," replied the Okhrana agent.

He managed to retrieve a pack of Pall Mall from his pocket. Mrs. Saint-Albray, acting as if she was handling a piece of garbage, took it and lit it at the flame of Rossiysky' lighter.

Without looking back, Kougloff said:

"No guardian angels, back there."

"Seems that way," replied Rossiysky, nodding his head.

Instead of crossing the border at the San Ysidro checkpoint, they turned left on the Via Internacional, planning to use the more discreet station at Los Laureles.

As they passed Calle Faustino Galicia, a Renault heading north made a too wide turn and hit their right rear fender.

The shock was barely noticeable, but enough to cause some damage to the two cars.

Kougloff braked. The driver of the other vehicle slowed more brusquely, and stopped three or four yards behind them. He left his car and walked towards Kougloff.

"It's totally my fault," he admitted spontaneously. "I hope I haven't damaged your fender too much."

He and Kougloff went to assess the effects of the accident. They leaned forward and, suddenly, the other driver struck the nape of Kougloff's neck with the edge of his hand.

The Okhrana agent collapsed to his knees. Then, his attacker hit him again, in the same place, with rage.

A second man, whose presence had been carefully hidden inside the other car, rapidly got out of it and quickly picked up Kougloff's body, while his colleague, pistol in hand, approached Rossiysky, who had just noticed something was wrong.

Stuck in front of Mrs. Saint-Albray, the Russian could not escape when the door opened. He raised his elbow to protect himself, but could not avoid being struck with the butt of the gun on the parietal bone and being immediately rendered unconscious.

After tying Rossiysky's wrists and ankles and lying him down on the back seat, the man got behind the wheel while Mrs. Saint-Albray sat next to him. He turned the Traction around and drove back towards Tijuana.

"*Gracias a dios!* We almost missed you!" said Alfredo—for it was he. "Luckily, I was right thinking that they'd go for the border but avoid San Ysidro."

Behind them, Manuel drove the Renault with Kougloff inside, accelerating to remain in Alfredo's wake.

"I really thought that you'd lost me," confessed Mrs. Saint-Albray, her heart pounding. "this country has become unhealthy for me."

"They're American agents," replied Alfredo, tense. "Zakuski's death seems to have triggered some kind of investigation, but we're not sure how, or why."

In front, Alfredo put his arm out the window to signal Manuel to slow down. They didn't want to risk being stopped by a traffic cop.

Both cars were now driving towards Camino Verde. Rather than taking Route 1, the Mexican used smaller roads crossing gloomy neighborhoods, where it was easier to detect and lose any possible followers.

Eventually, they arrived at a *chatarreria*, a junkyard filled with car wrecks.

The Renault stopped, while Alfredo drove the Traction into the junkyard.

"Let's get out," he told Mrs. Saint-Albray, "and move the kid. The owner of this junkyard will get rid of the Traction for us."

In no time, Rossiysky's body was transferred to the Renault and curled up next to Kougloff's. A blanket was summarily thrown over them. Mrs. Saint-Albray sat in the front, while Alfredo managed to squeeze his athletic body onto the back seat, putting his feet on the two Russians, ready to knock them out again if they began to move.

Manuel started the car and they again took to the road, generally avoiding major avenues until they reached the same dilapidated restaurant where Trump had been taken prisoner.

"*Dios mio!*" muttered Manuel. "We're there! I half-expected we'd be arrested by the police!"

CHAPTER XVIII

"One thing for sure, you can't go back to the Hilton," said Alfredo to Mrs. Saint-Albray.

"Or to the U.S.," she added with bitterness. "What am I going to do…?"

"Requesón will provide you with a new identity," cut in Alfredo. "The bottom line is that you've managed to escape. Anyway, your mission was almost finished. It will all work out, you'll see."

Daylight did nothing to improve the dilapidated restaurant where Trump had unsuccessfully fought for his freedom two nights before. It was a shabby brick building, painted deep red, its windows boarded over with planks, its facade pockmarked by machine gun fire.

They got out of the Renault. Alfredo went to open the door while Manuel removed the blanket that was covering the two Russian agents.

The two men were still unconscious, their complexions sallow.

The Mexican looked around, then called his sidekick:

"Alfredo, come help me. We'll drag them inside."

Handing his gun to Mrs. Saint-Albray, so she could cover the two agents if they awoke, Alfredo helped Manuel transport them inside.

The operation went smoothly. The two unconscious agents were unceremoniously thrown into the dungeon-like cell where Trump was being kept.

"The damp down there will do them good," Alfredo snickered, slightly out of breath because of the effort involved.

The trio met back in the kitchen cellar. Manuel uncorked a bottle of tequila and filled three glasses.

Mrs. Saint-Albray emptied hers in a single gulp.

"What happened last night?" she inquired, her face tense. "Was the man following me another FBI agent?"

"CIA, actually," replied Manuel, wiping his mouth with the back of the hand. "Requesón seems inclined to believe him."

"Then, the first one must also have been CIA or FBI," murmured the young woman, her eyes unfocused, not noticing the look of complicity exchanged by her two associates. "But why have the American authorities suddenly decided to arrest me—in Tijuana, of all places?"

"So far, we don't know," pronounced Alfredo, approaching her. "What is sure is that we smell a rat. Maybe we should all have a good time before we're forced to pack our bags and take off, right, Monique?"

She quickly looked up at him and saw an evil glint of desire in his eyes.

"You owe us, right?" Manuel added with a lascivious smile. "Without us, you'd be in a *yanqui* jail."

He unbuttoned Mrs. Saint-Albray's coat, staring into her eyes. Appalled, she recoiled slightly, but hit the edge of the table.

"You're crazy!" she protested. "This isn't the time to…"

"Why not?" Alfredo said, sarcastically, stroking her upper thigh with a caressing hand. It's not like we haven't already had a lot of fun here. And it's quiet, we won't be disturbed…"

Manuel moved the glasses, depositing them near the stove. Alfredo undid Mrs. Saint-Albray's raincoat.

"No," she said, clearly furious. "What do you take me for? You're crazy!"

"Shut your trap," replied Alfredo, coarsely. "After following you all this time, we've gotten turned on. You need to be nice to your guardian angels, eh, *chica*?"

With a ruthless grip, he pushed her back on the table. Then, Manuel held her by the shoulders and began to hungrily kiss her on the lips,

Monique used all her strength to try to kick Alfredo with her feet. Suffocating under Manuel's forced kisses, she heard the other Mexican laugh.

Her ankles were now trapped by a pair of steel fingers, and roughly pushed apart.

She felt her underwear being ripped aside; her heart quickened as Alfredo closed his hands around her waist; then she felt the odious, invasive, painful penetration that quickly followed.

"You can let her go now," whispered Alfredo, in drunken satisfaction, a few minutes later. "Let's switch."

Manuel stopped biting Mrs. Saint-Albray's mouth and took his associate's place, while the other man stepped back. There was no longer any need to keep her in place, as she lay there, defeated and in despair.

With a lump in his throat, his temples throbbing, Alfredo calmed his impatience by lighting a cigarette, waiting for Manuel to finish raping the woman.

Afterward, Mrs. Saint-Albray sat up and shook her hair loose.

Alfredo stood in one corner of the room, his back turned. Smiling, Manuel shamelessly ogled the elegant underwear that had been tossed aside on the floor.

Having restored some order in her clothes, Mrs. Saint-Albray hissed angrily:

"You two are bastards! I'll get you back for this."

"You've got nothing to complain about," Alfredo said in a mocking tone. "Unless you want another go?"

"Leave me alone!" she snarled back. "You should get Requesón. We need to talk. Then you can go back to your whores."

Alfredo faced her and chuckled:

"Don't put yourself down, *chica.*"

With his simplistic mentality, he thought she had to be promiscuous just because she was involved in some kind of clandestine business. He never would have believed her if she had told him the opposite was true. But she didn't tell him because she knew that the idea of having raped a good woman would only have further increased his pleasure.

"Let's get out of here," she insisted, retying her scarf. "There are decisions to be made, especially for me. Pulling me out of the clutches of the Americans isn't enough. There are other problems to solve!"

"Let's go then," Alfredo approved.

He felt good. He looked at Mrs. Saint-Albray with a complacent eye, then nodded to Manuel.

All three walked out. A heavy rain pattered on the roof of the car.

The Renault drove away, throwing splatters of mud in its wake.

CHAPTER XIX

Donald J. Trump, who had trembled like a little boy upon hearing the huge door of his cell turn on its hinges, failed to catch the unconscious Kougloff when the man was thrown in the middle of a puddle.

A minute later, the body of Rossiysky also tumbled onto the soggy ground. But the dense darkness prevented Trump from recognizing the two Okhrana agents.

Not knowing who the unfortunate prisoners doomed to share his captivity were, he spoke to them. Getting no response, as the newcomers were not moving, he wondered if they weren't merely corpses that had been temporarily dumped into the cellar.

Hungry, moisture oozing from his mouth, not having slept since the day before because of the rats rummaging around, Trump crawled near one of the bodies and felt the clothes and the figure of the man lying on the ground.

He was warm, his heart was beating. He was unconscious, maybe injured, but alive.

Fearing he would catch a cold if his clothes became soaked, Trump lifted the man's torso and dragged him towards the opposite wall. As uncomfortable as it was, it at least had the merit of being dry. He sat the man down and patted his face.

Behind him, he heard a groan. Leaning on his hands, his eyes open, but seeing absolutely nothing. For a minute, Rossiysky thought that he had gone blind. His head ached horribly.

"Kougloff..." he groaned, still dazed.

Trump's heart twitched when he recognized the voice.

"Rossiysky? Is that you?"he asked hoarsely.

Scanning the darkness in vain, the young officer stammered:

"Yes... Yes, it's me... Who are you?"

"It's Trump! So I guess the other guy is Kougloff?"

"Yes! We were together. We were attacked on the road. Where are we? I can't see anything."

Excruciating anxiety choked his voice.

"Neither can I," said Trump. "It's dark as shit in here. I've had time to get used to it since yesterday, but I can't even see my own fingers when I hold them in front of my eyes."

He approached Rossiysky and touched him.

"Are you hurt? If so, try not to touch the wound. This place is full of germs."

"One of them knocked me unconscious with the butt of his gun," painfully uttered the Russian. "I'm still dazed."

"Try to stand up, otherwise you'll be bitten by the rats. They took off when you guys were thrown in here, but they'll be back."

"*Prokljatie!*" uttered Rossiysky, suddenly revived.

He made an effort to follow Trump's advice, grabbed the American and managed to stand up on his own two legs.

"What about Kougloff?" he asked anxiously. "How is he?"

"Knocked out, like you were," Trump replied. "Only Kostromskoy is still missing. God knows what's happened to him!"

Rossiysky, searching his pockets, unearthed his lighter. He lit it. The low flame dissipated the darkness. Some shapes were now outlined, including the profiles of the prisoners.

"Don't waste your fuel," said Trump. "We might need that lighter later."

" I had to be sure," replied Rossiysky, turning it off. "OK, my eyes work."

Then his thoughts returned to his boss.

"They didn't kill him, did they?"

"Who? Kostromskoy? I don't know."

"No, Kougloff. He's still not moving."

Trump returned to the Russian and shook him gently, calling him by his name.

Kougloff finally emitted a grunt and, with his arm, tried to wave away the American. Trump finished bringing him back to consciousness:

"Come on, take a deep breath, man. I know it doesn't smell like vintage *Triumf*, but you need some air. Stay awake. And don't panic; it's dark in here."

He guessed more than saw the painful grimace that Kougloff made when he belched:

"Are we in Hell?"

"Maybe not far from it. I'm Trump. Rossiysky is standing next to me, not too badly damaged. But things look bad. Best case scenario, we may be locked in here for some time yet."

Kougloff meditated on these words, as he fought to regain his senses. His voice finally rose in the sepulchral silence:

"How were you captured?"

"They took me by surprise," said Trump. "I think they had planned exactly what they were going to do since they first spotted Kostromskoy. They knew we were going to follow Saint-Albray, but at a safe distance. They must have been monitoring the metro exit at Rosarito, and spotted me right away. They arrested me, pretending to be DIS agents, but that's obviously a lie. And you, how did you end up here?"

Kougloff brought Trump up to date on their recent odyssey.

"What a disaster!" grumbled the American. "The odd thing is, they don't seem to know much. Their boss interrogated me, and his questions were all over the place. Strange as it seems, they asked me why I was following Mrs. Saint-Albray."

"What did you tell them?"

"Nothing really, but I hinted I was working for the CIA, monitoring suspicious doings by Americans in Mexico. They didn't seem particularly troubled by that."

"Did they mention Kostromskoy?"

"Barely. They don't seem better informed about his role than my own. In fact, I wonder if they actually interrogated him…"

A silence enveloped the three prisoners.

Groping around, Kougloff sought some place to prop himself in order to get up. He felt the cold slowly invading his limbs.

Rossiysky plunged his hands into his pockets, hoping to find his cigarettes. He extricated them from his overcoat and blindly offered them around.

"Cigarettes?" he suggested. "I still have a few left."

"God, yes!" said Trump, accepting by feeling though the darkness around him. "Maybe it'll soothe my stomach cramps. I'm starved.

Rossiysky's lighter illuminated the walls, revealing their putrid filth. The light briefly flared when all three men drew in the first puffs, then the darkness returned and closed over them.

"They're bound to interrogate us again," said Kougloff. "What should we tell them?"

Trump, who had not told Kougloff the origins of the case, suggested:

"Let's stick to my story: we're all American agents; I'm CIA; you're FBI. Why not? We've been ordered to monitor, and possibly arrest, Monique Saint-Albray who is suspected of some kind of trafficking. No more, no less. They don't have any reason to suspect the Okhrana is involved."

Rossiysky intervened:

"What if we tried to escape? We don't want to rot here."

"Wait," Kougloff said. "I still want to get a few things straight... Whose hands are we in? Why aren't we in a regular Mexican jail?"

"Because obviously," said Trump, "these people, Saint-Albray included, are working against the Mexican Empire."

"What?" said Rossiysky, dumbfounded.

"Yeah, think about it," confirmed Trump. "They're in hiding; that's undeniable. Why didn't they take us to the DIS or the local authorities, unless they were working against them?"

Trump had come up with another reason, but one which he didn't share. Initially, it was the French who had pulled the alarm on this case. They were still allies of the Mexican Empire. Perhaps Colonel Roquefort had been trying to use the Okhrana to stop a secret rebel movement that opposed the Mexican Imperial regime without showing his hand?

Wheels within wheels.

Kougloff said:

"I hope you're right. It might be our best chance to get out of here."

"I think so, too," said Trump, puffing on his cigarette and making it glow again. "Still, if we can slip away, as Rossiysky suggested, we shouldn't hesitate. But it seems to me that the prospects of success are slim."

"Let's see," said Rossiysky, with the ineradicable hope of youth. "We are three now."

"Yes," Trump admitted. "The trouble is that there is no window and only a ram could break down that door."

CHAPTER XX

Meanwhile, another secret meeting was being held in the back of the photo store in Rosarito.

The two Mexican gunmen were reporting the events of the morning to their chief, Requesón, but without mentioning their "private entertainment."

Mrs. Saint-Albray stood to the side, glowering, her face pale and tired.

Upset, Requesón bit his lower lip.

"This is a disaster," he said. "Mrs. Saint-Albray is now definitely burned on the American side. Her help will be difficult to replace, but that's not the worst. Now we have to find a way to clear her name with the DIS and the DGSS."[4].

"And urgently!" added Mrs. Saint-Albray. "I'm in far more danger than you and I'm getting tired of this. There isn't going to be anywhere in the world where I can be safe if word of this spreads. It's time you get things sorted."

"We're trying as hard as we can," Requesón retorted in a sharp voice. "But we don't have the men, the time or the resources. I can't solve all the problems by

---

[4] *Direction Générale des Services Spéciaux*. French intelligence agency.

myself. If Zakuski hadn't been so stupid, we wouldn't be in this shit."

Mrs. Saint-Albray fell silent.

The mention of Pavel Zakuski's death had echoed in her mind as an alarm signal. That had started the whole mess, which continued to deteriorate. But who was behind it all?

Why had Requesón been late for their appointment?

"...Anyway," continued the latter, less acerbic, "an ID change, new papers and some cosmetic modifications to your appearance will help with your relocation. Maybe Brazil? You wouldn't be exposed to anything unpleasant there. Your luggage is at the Hilton. I'll talk to a travel agency that's worked with us in the past, and they'll pick it up and send it on. We'll wipe your tracks. This is the most urgent. For the rest, I guess you're not in a hurry, right?"

"No," she agreed. "I can leave you with some instructions regarding my home in Los Angeles. I shouldn't be concerned with it now; it's part of my old life. I guess I always knew I would be forced to leave once my mission was over. When do I leave?"

"In no more than two weeks, I promise. A truck will take you to Ciudad del Panama. There, you can board a steamer to Salvador de Bahia. After that, you'll be on your own. But we're not ingrates. You'll get a handsome sum of money upon departure."

"Where am I going to stay in the meantime?"

"At the Adria, a hotel in Ensenada run by one of our associates. It's better, I think, that you cut off all contact with anyone, including us. One last question: is there anything left in Los Angeles that might compromise us?"

"Nothing except the infrared telescope, and I doubt anyone will guess what I was using it for."

Requesón nodded.

"Don't underestimate the shrewdness of the Americans. After all, what was the clue that led them to you?"

Mrs. Saint-Albray didn't answer. The Mexican continued:

"Let's leave it behind; the game isn't worth the effort. Besides, they might catch my agent just like they caught Poshekhonsky. Do you have enough money on you?"

"Enough to get by for now. Will you take care of my company? What about my other assets?"

There was so much bitterness in her voice that Requesón realized that she was having second thoughts.

"Don't be depressed, Monique," he spoke with a sudden benevolence. "Abandoning everything that you own is obviously a big sacrifice, but your freedom, your safety, is paramount. A clever lawyer who works for us in Los Angeles will make sure that your company is sold for a good price, and the money will be sent to you in Brazil in ways no one can detect. But I don't think that the Americans have filed any specific charges against you, so you shouldn't worry. Count on me, I'll do my best to limit the damage."

Mrs. Saint-Albray, however, remained concerned. The notion of leaving the United States forever was, for her, a disaster, even if most of her personal fortune could be saved.

"What will you do with your prisoners?" she asked in a bleak tone.

Requesón made a throat slitting gesture.

"We need to protect ourselves at every step. They're of no use to us. In fact, they represent a threat. So we'll eliminate them."

Alfredo and Manuel silently exchanged a knowing look. They would likely be responsible for this unpleasant task.

Before deciding to leave, Mrs. Saint-Albray said:

"You know, Señor Requesón, I sometimes wonder if we didn't take on a task that's beyond our abilities. Even if things go as planned tonight, do you think it will have a decisive effect?"

The Mexican stiffened.

"We will continue to strike for as long as it takes," he scowled, "even if we fail this time. Millions of people live only because they hope for a better future, free of Imperial tyranny, and we would be the worst of cowards if we gave up now. Our faith in the final victory must be unshakable!"

He hammered his words with a fanatical belief that impressed his subordinates as well as Mrs. Saint-Albray. An iron will animated this curious character, who looked so meek and ordinary to the rest of the world.

His diatribe revived the failing convictions of the Frenchwoman.

"I'll do what you say. I'll watch the news tonight, and I'll know if you have a marked a point. Goodbye, Señor Requesón."

She shook his hand, then walked out, without giving Alfredo and Manuel the least sign of recognition.

After she had left the store, Requesón considered his acolytes with such attention that they felt very uncomfortable. Then, without commentary, he continued:

"Here's how I planned our action tonight…"

CHAPTER XXI

Around eight o'clock, Alfredo and Manuel returned to the abandoned restaurant, but instead of entering it, they circled the building and walked into a backlot that had not been maintained for at least fifteen years.

They stepped over rubble and garbage, avoided bits of barbed wire, and finally reached a ramshackle wooden shed, which had previously been used to store tools.

Alfredo took a key from his pocket and opened the rusty padlock that kept the cracked wood panel used as a door shut. By the light of a flashlight held by Manuel, the two men went inside.

Alfredo kicked aside the miscellaneous debris that was lying on the ground, then lifted an old, empty crate. Under it was a water valve connected to an underground pipe.

The Mexican tried to turn it. It was stuck, forcing him to use all of his strength. Grinning, despite his bruised fingers, he forced it to make a quarter turn, and then another, increasing the water flow.

"If they're thirsty, they'll appreciate the water," he cackled, putting the crate back on top of the valve.

Manuel added:

"In their own way, they were helpful to the cause. Their disappearance is bound to stir up a lot of trouble for the Empire."

"American bastards!" Alfredo hissed. "They're worse than the French! I hope they rot in Hell!"

The two men walked back outside, re-locking the door behind them. Then they returned to their car and immediately drove off.

Leaving Camino Verde and retracing their journey, they reached La Joya less than an hour later, and drove towards the outskirts of Tijuana, where the skeletal shells of factories remained in the middle of an industrial wasteland. Here and there stood a working plant or warehouse, miraculously spared by the blight. It was the middle of the night and no one stirred in the alleyways of this gloomy industrial cemetery.

Alfredo stopped the car in the courtyard of one of the abandoned factories, its machinery long since shipped to Asia or South America. They waited inside, since they were ahead of schedule.

An hour later, a two-ton truck, its back covered by a tarpaulin, arrived in relative silence. The driver parked in a particularly dark corner and turned off the lights.

Alfredo and Manuel went to meet the new arrivals: Requesón and a forty-year-old man with a worried face.

"This is Cotija," said Requesón laconically, pointing to his companion. "Come on, there's no time to lose."

While Alfredo and Manuel set up a metal ramp at the back of the truck, Requesón removed the pins that held the back of the tarpaulin, and climbed under it. Cotija followed him and, together, they rolled out a metal contraption five feet high and one a half feet wide that looked something like a stepladder with the sides encased in a metal box.

Alfredo and Manuel helped unload the machine.

Together, they carried it inside the deserted factory, then used a freight elevator to take it to the roof.

The roof overlooked the southern section of Tijuana, with unimpeded view of Cuauhtemoc International Airport. slightly to the northeast, it's lights twinkling in the darkness.

But Alfredo and Manuel wasted no time contemplating the panorama. Out of breath and perspiring, they laid down their burden. After a brief pause, they went back to the courtyard without much enthusiasm.

A second package was waiting for them: an oblong object, three feet long with a square base about one foot wide.

"Watch out!" recommended Requesón. "It's heavy!"

Thanks to the joint efforts of the four men, the box was carefully unloaded from the truck.

Alfredo and Manuel then grabbed it and began their second trip to the roof, while Requesón and Cotija grabbed various accessories, including a rubberized roll of wire.

All this equipment was taken to the rooftop terrace. There, Cotija began to work: Using a compass, he determined the direction of the airport, which allowed the final positioning of the projectile's ramp. Then, while his three companions were dismantling the crate, he unrolled a few meters of wire and checked the contacts soldered to the two conductors.

Their activities took place in absolute silence and darkness, each man knowing by heart the details of his task.

After an hour, a ground-to-air missile was placed inside its cradle, tilted at forty-five degrees, its nose pointed towards the starless sky.

"Now you can go," muttered Requesón to his two acolytes. "I'll do the rest."

Alfredo and Manuel didn't need to be told twice. They disappeared down the elevator and rushed to their car.

Soon, the Renault discreetly drove away from the factory.

Meanwhile, Cotija had finished unwinding cable. He dropped its end over the roof guard down to the ground. Having wedged a loop of the cable under the machine, he connected the conductors to the firing pins.

After carefully checking the installation, he said to Requesón:

"It's all set. Once I'm down, I'll only need two or three minutes. Let's go."

They left the roof terrace, took the freight elevator down, and once again arrived in the courtyard.

Cotija walked along the factory wall to reach the end of the cable. When he did, he grabbed it and carefully pulled on it to get the length he wanted, then, although he felt his stomach knotted by jitters, he connected the stripped ends to a box that Requesón was holding.

"Now we just need to wait for zero hour," he muttered. "I hope your information is good and nothing happens to upset our plan."

"Unless fate takes a hand, all should be fine," affirmed his companion. "No offense, but my biggest worry is a technical problem."

Cotija shook his head.

"Nah. It'll be fine. I know what I'm doing." He consulted the phosphorescent dial of his wristwatch. "I have 3:30 a.m. What about you?"

"The same. Get ready."

They listened carefully to the diffuse sounds that sometimes broke through the darkness: a train traveling south, the far-off horn of a ship on the ocean, the buzz of a plane flying at high altitude.

Against this muddled background, they were waiting for a very specific noise. It came; at first, a faint note, but growing in intensity as it became a true clamor.

"Here it comes," announced Requesón, his lips dry.

The rumble was that of the four engines of a Latécoère 915 weighing over a hundred tons, yet defying Earth's gravity and roaring with colossal power as it took off from Cuauhtemoc International Airport.

The two Mexicans saw the plane's lights blinking regularly as it gained altitude, flying over the southern section of Camino Verde.

Cotija, his heart pounding, pressed the contact.

On the roof terrace, a burst of flame flared from the back of the rocket. The ground-to-air missile flew up its ramp and charged towards the Latécoère.

Requesón and his accomplice, fascinated, saw the light formed by the missile's incandescent propulsion gases describe an uncertain trajectory as it zigzagged, then suddenly stabilized and flew implacably toward the heated engines of the jet overhead.

The missile plunged like a bird of prey onto the rear of the plane, and, for a split second, seemed to merge with its lights. Then, a violent explosion lit the huge plane, which disintegrated in mid-flight. While two of its engines continued to spit flames, fragments of the hull and pieces of the wing scattered in the dark, then fell to the ground in a fiery rain.

Requesón nervous hand squeezed Cotija's.

"We did it!" he growled triumphantly. "Come, let's get out of here!"

Cotija feverishly unfastened the cable from the box. He was running toward the truck just as two loud thumps made the air vibrate. A few hundred yards away, the debris of the Latécoère had crashed to earth.

The two terrorists could easily get out of danger before anyone could locate the place from where the missile had originated, even assuming that someone had noticed it, especially since the scene of the crash itself would first capture all the attention.

Requesón maneuvered the truck without turning on the headlights. After a quick check in both directions, the vehicle hit the road. Once he was sure they were safe, the Mexican pressed on the accelerator and turned on the lights.

Despite all the ambulances, the sirens of which could already be heard screeching through the darkness, none of the passengers traveling on Imperial Mexican Airline flight 057 to Paris that night would ever reach their destination.

CHAPTER XXII

It hadn't taken long for Donald J. Trump and his colleagues to stop talking. After an initial period of excitement, they experienced the first symptoms of discouragement. The oppressive quality of the darkness into which they were plunged would have shaken the nerves of even the toughest individual.

Moreover, they were tortured by hunger, and although they had periodically done some stretching exercises to warm up, they remained bitterly cold.

It was Rossiysky who was the first to notice an unusual hissing sound. At first, he paid it little attention; but, feeling frustrated at not identifying its source, he said:

"Do either of you hear anything? It sounds like water, and the ground definitely feels wetter than before."

Kougloff broke his silence.

"You're right! Where is it coming from?"

"Maybe it's raining outside?" said Trump. "At least, we'll be dry in here."

Rossiysky raised his face toward a ceiling, the existence of which he could only guess, then turned his head to the right, then to the left. It seemed to him that this discreet sound came from a corner of the cell, at a height of about ten feet.

He walked to the spot, ran his fingers over the stones, and detected a trickle of water that dripped down the wall.

"No mistake," he announced, with wet hands. "The water is coming from here."

"Call a plumber," Trump said, ineptly trying to crack a joke. "I've always said, this room lacks the most rudimentary comfort."

Rossiysky, disinclined to make fun of their predicament, replied:

"I hope that this water can go somewhere else, otherwise we'll soon be wading in it."

Indeed, the flow rate had increased and now the gurgling sound above their heads had become much louder.

"If it's a leak in a pipe," theorized Kougloff, "there must also be a drain hole."

"The ground isn't even either," pointed out Trump. "The puddles are two inches deep over here."

"It's worse where I am," noted Rossiysky. "I have water up to my ankles. And I don't think there's a drain.

In the silence that followed, everyone wondered about the risk created by this new factor.

"When are they going to get us out of here?" Rossiysky grumbled. "Good God, why leave us in this dump! If they wanted to kill us, they could have done it already."

Trump felt a shudder through his entire being. He remembered the noise the door had made when closing—exactly that of a watertight door the edges of which were lined with a rubber gasket.

So the cell was designed to hold water. And the door's thickness was adequate enough to withstand high pressure...

He could not share the awful suspicion that had just grabbed hold of him.

Kougloff's impassive voice rose above the sound of the water:

"In my opinion, this isn't rain pouring into our dungeon, Rossiysky."

"No?"

"No. This is the first time you've seen this water since you've been here, isn't it, Mr. Trump?"

"Yes. I would have noticed it if it had happened when I was alone."

An almost palpable anguish settled in the hollow silence.

"You... you think they want to drown us?" Rossiysky asked fearfully.

"We'll find out soon enough when we see how fast the level rises."

Rossiysky lit his lighter and bent down. Then he took a knife from his pocket and drew a mark on the wall, five feet above the water.

"This cellar is approximately one hundred and twenty square feet," clarified Trump. "I measured it last night. A rise of two inches would mean an inflow of 160 gallons. At that rate, we'll still be around for a while."

Kougloff understood that this was not to comfort Rossiysky, only emphasizing that their agony might last.

"Let's use whatever time we have left," Rossiysky suggested. "What if we plug that pipe?"

"That's no solution," grumbled Trump. "There's only one answer: we have to escape. Starving or freezing to death is no better than drowning or asphyxiation."

"*Da*, but how? You yourself said that our chances were nil."

"I still think that, but what other choice do we have? Our foes have decided to eliminate us, so we have to break out of here through a hole in the wall. Do you have a knife, Kougloff?"

"Yes. A pretty solid one, too."

"Mine is a Spanish Army knife," intervened Rossiysky. "Maybe I can loosen a stone…"

"Let's think first," Trump said. "We're probably twelve or thirteen feet underground. We should dig the wall as high as possible in order to make an oblique passage toward the surface.

"You think we can get out that way?" inquired Kougloff.

"Yes, because unless I'm mistaken, this cell is located under some kind of courtyard. I followed a long corridor before being thrown in here."

"Why not drill directly through the ceiling?" suggested Rossiysky.

"Because it's out of our reach. Let's start with a methodical inspection. If we discover a damaged part of the wall, that will make things easier. Climb on my shoulders, Rossiysky, and we can examine the dungeon."

In the dark, they approached one another. Trump leaned against the wall and made a ladder with his hands.

"Wait a minute," said Rossiysky. "I'll take off my shoes. They're unnecessary for what we're going to do."

Seconds later, he climbed on Trump's hands, then on his shoulders. Leaning with one hand on the wall, he flicked his lighter again and explored the rough surface of the walls, trying to assess their hardness. The upper portion didn't look the same as its bottom. At the bottom, there were only large, irregular stones, joined by cement. Near the top, a uniform layer of concrete covered the wall, both horizontally and vertically.

"It feels like concrete," grumbled Rossiysky. "I wonder if we're inside an old bunker…"

The light flickered.

Grabbing Rossiysky by his ankles, Trump moved slowly to the left.

"I couldn't see the ceiling," said Kougloff, "even though you held your lighter above your head. Trump, could you stretch a little more? Rossiysky, can you feel it with your hand?"

Rossiysky tried, but even on tiptoe, his fingers only brushed the vertical wall.

"Nothing," he announced. "I can't touch it." The flame flickered again. "It's not a knife we need, but a pneumatic drill. I can't feel any cracks."

"Try again! Just one is all we need," said Trump, without moving his head. "It's always easier to enlarge an existing hole than create a new one."

"*Da*," agreed Kougloff. "But before continuing your search, it might be worth checking something else…"

"What?" asked Trump.

The Russian added soon after:

"What if we are locked inside a tank?"

CHAPTER XXIII

Rossiysky climbed down from his human ladder, found himself with his feet submerged in freezing water, and sneezed.

"*Vot eto pizdets!*" he grumbled, wiping his nose. "I'm going to catch my death in here!" he added, without a trace of irony.

"I see what you mean," Donald J. Trump said, responding to Kougloff. "A tank would usually be topped with a metal plate of some kind, right?"

"*Da.* Perhaps it is up there, above our heads, inaccessible for a single prisoner, but not for three. It would be easier to lift that than to dig a tunnel through the ground."

"That would be perfect," noted Trump, sententiously. "Rossiysky, get back up on my shoulders. Kougloff, climb up on him and try reaching the ceiling."

The Okhrana agent could not help smiling.

"I have not made a human pyramid since my gym class days at the Academy," he warned. "It's going to be almost impossible to keep our balance in the dark, but I'll try."

I'll lean against the wall for support," said Trump. "And when you reach the top, push against the ceiling. I won't move until you tell me."

Kougloff got rid of his overcoat, which would only make him heavier and less mobile. Trump, standing as firmly as possible, clasped his hands. Rossiysky, already accustomed to the routine, climbed first, and managed to stand on the shoulders of the American, Then he, too, leaned against the wall.

"Ready!"" he announced to Kougloff. "Your turn."

Kougloff grabbed the younger man and tried to gain a foothold stepping onto Trump's shoulders. Rossiysky clasped his hands and Kougloff stepped onto the cradle formed by the interlaced fingers, and finally, grabbing Rossiysky's shoulders, he raised himself up.

There was a loud thud and a Russian curse.

"My head!" moaned Kougloff, wobbling.

He had banged his head against the ceiling, and the shock and pain had almost caused him to fall.

It took him a few seconds to recover, meanwhile he muttered:

"At least I found the ceiling."

Trump, supporting the weight of the two agents, gripped Rossiysky by his calves, to strengthen the balance of their living column. At the top, almost sitting on Rossiysky's head, was Kougloff, the palms of his hands meticulously exploring the ceiling. He moved them inch by inch, while Trump carefully stepped forward.

With feverish ardor, he explored in every direction.

"Stop!" he suddenly shouted.

Without letting go of the spot he had found, he managed to retrieve his own lighter from his pocket with his other hand. After three failed attempts, the wick flared.

"There is a cover!" he exclaimed. "A little to the right... It's circular... Made of stone!"

Trump, whose legs began to tremble under the strain imposed upon them, took one slow step forward, then another.

"Perfect!" threw Kougloff. "Hold on tight now. I'm going to try to lift it."

The additional pressure almost crushed Trump, but he was a big man. Clenching his jaws, he contracted his muscles. He felt dizzy because of hunger and his longer stay in the icy dungeon.

"Hurry up!" he gasped, his veins swelling.

A rough sound echoed above him.

Panting, Kougloff finished pushing against the stone cover. A breath of fresh air caressed his face as it opened. His fingers, like grappling hooks, clung to the edge of the aperture and, with a last effort, he hauled himself up. Waving his feet with frantic force, he launched himself out of the hole and managed to crawl to escape, his hands clutching at the dirty soil around him..

A notable reduction in weight relieved Trump, destabilized by Rossiysky's involuntary movements.

"Kougloff is out!" said Rossiysky, stunned to see a clear circle of pale light above his head. "It's fantastic!"

"Get down," ordered Trump. "Give me a break."

Rossiysky knelt down, then jumped and landed feet first in the rising water.

A shadow appeared in the opening above them.

"We're safe!" said Kougloff. "I think that the building is empty; I don't see any light. Now I'll get a rope to pull you up."

His teeth chattered, maybe because of the excitement, or the cold.

"Hurry up!" enjoined Trump. "The Mexicans could return at any time."

"*Da!*" said Kougloff, who disappeared.

The Russian agent looked around him, and spotted the shed at the opposite end of the courtyard. He ran toward it on the uneven ground, tripping on some of the garbage.

The sight of the padlock annoyed him, sparking a reaction of pure rage. Wedging his heels into the ground, he pulled the makeshift door towards him with all his force, angrily shaking the rotten panel. Cracking noises resounded; one of them louder than the others, while the Okhrana agent tore the door loose.

Feeling warmer now, Kougloff stepped inside the shed and looked for a rope strong enough to withstand the weight of a man.

But all he saw was a bunch of tools and miscellaneous objects; there was no rope. Looking in a crate, he frowned at the sight of a valve which apparently had no reason to exist. He closed his hand over it and swung it both ways; realizing that it was open, he turned it off, then again began to look for a rope.

Apprehension crept into him. How could he believe that he would so easily find a strong rope essential to release his friends?

Furious, he left the shed and returned to the tank.

"Don't think I'm fooling around up here," he said, leaning over the opening. "I still can't find a rope."

"A pole or a ladder would do do just fine," said Trump. "Incidentally, the water has stopped flowing."

"*Da.* I found the valve and shut it off. Don't worry, I'll be right back."

As he walked away, the sound of an explosion shattered the calm of the night.

Awe-struck, Kougloff looked up. His eyes swept the night sky and in the west, they saw two large shooting stars, low on the horizon.

There was a crashing sound, then silence reigned once again.

With more important worries than pondering about this celestial phenomenon, Kougloff approached the back of the building that had once been a restaurant.

Cautious, he walked around it quietly, making sure it was really deserted. The windows were all dark and there was no sign of life.

Concerned that he was still unable to find a rope, he reconsidered the problem: since he had stopped the water from flowing into the tank, and since the building was deserted, it was easier to free his two comrades from inside the house by opening the door.

Kougloff didn't hesitate. With his elbow, he broke a pane of glass in a rear window and, running his hand between the fragments still stuck in the grooves, he maneuvered the catch.

Once inside, he crossed the storage room, found the main hall, then the stairs to the basement. At the bottom was a dilapidated kitchen where he made a short stop in the hope of finding a box of matches.

He found one near the stove, then went in search of the long underground corridor which Trump had mentioned.

It wasn't hard to find. He struck a match, held it in the air to recon the location, then moved forward in the dark, one arm held out in front of him.

After twenty yards, he made a turn and, a few steps away, his fingers encountered a frozen metal surface. A second match allowed him to see that it was the enormous armored door with its huge bolts.

"It's just me!" he shouted as he released the bolts and began to pull the door open.

Two exclamations of joy greeted his call; three seconds later, he barely had enough time to press against the wall to avoid being hit by Trump as he rushed out.

He lit several more matches in order to show them the way outside.

"Come into the kitchen, there's no one home."

In a dead run, the three men fled their dreadful prison.

In the kitchen, guided by his gluttonous instincts, Trump found a bottle of tequila and a few pieces of sugar stuck to the bottom of an earthenware bowl.

While Kougloff kept watch, Trump and Rossiysky rubbed their feet with alcohol to get them warm again.

"And now," Trump said between clenched teeth, "we have a mighty score to settle!"

CHAPTER XXIV

It was five a.m. when Donald J. Trump and the two Okhrana agents finally left the building through the rear exit.

Before departing, Trump had made sure they re-sealed the tank and relocked the security door to the deadly cellar. If the Mexicans came back, it was better for them to not realize too quickly that their captives escaped.

For the same reason, they had reluctantly decided to leave behind Kougloff's Traction Avant, which was still parked in the courtyard.

As they briskly walked through the dark, silent streets of the suburban neighborhood of Camino Verde, glad for the exercise, happy to breathe in the fresh air, Trump, his face overgrown with stubble, said:

"I don't think dear Mrs. Saint-Albray will have had the nerve to return to the Hilton. She knows that we've unmasked her. Our kidnapping made it even more dangerous for her. But I want to question her more than ever... That broad knows the truth."

"That bitch, you mean," corrected Rossiysky. "Ah, she really got us. You should have seen her act, playing the part of the persecuted innocent, while knowing full well that her killers were going to grab us."

"So what's the plan? Are we going back to your hotel?" asked Kougloff.

"For that, we need a car," said Trump.

"Want me to hot-wire one?" offered Rossiysky.

"No," said Trump. "If it gets reported, we could be stopped and be in trouble with the *Guardia*."

"Let's take the metro," proposed Kougloff. "The station isn't more than ten minutes on foot. And I still have enough Mexican Francs to buy us three tickets."

"Do you have any agent in the area who could put us up until the morning and loan us a car?" asked Trump.

Kougloff scratched his chin.

"Not close, no."

"We can't walk around in circles all night," grumbled Rossiysky. "Let me steal a car."

Trump reflected.

"No. It's too dangerous. Besides, I want to get to their boss before he realizes we're gone. I know their lair. It's in a photo shop in Rosarito. I can find it from the train station…"

They had just arrived at the corner of a long straight avenue, its perspective lost in the distance, bright with new street lighting.

Two police cars, rooftop lights flashing, appeared in the distance. The speed with which they drove indicated they were not on an ordinary patrol, but on their way to a specific destination.

The three men didn't change anything about their behavior, continuing to walk normally.

The cars crossed the intersection, turned right, and the intermittent flashes of their lights faded quickly.

Kougloff muttered:

"Something is going on. That's strange."

"Just our luck," commented Trump, disgusted. "Maybe we should just go for the metro…"

He was about to continue when, suddenly, an idea struck him.

"Wait a minute!" he exclaimed. "We can order a cab!"

"With what?" asked Kougloff.

Trump took his right shoe off, and rotated the elevator heel. Inside was an American Express card.

"I never leave home without it," he said, smiling, putting his shoe back on. "Let's find a pay phone, call a cab, and have him take us to a car rental place."

Dawn was rising over Rosarito. To the East, the sky was tinged with red clouds.

The area around the photo shop was deserted. There was no Renault parked nearby. As before, the store's iron curtain was shut, but one could easily enter the building either through its front door or a side door, since only a symbolic fence marked the boundaries between the street and an alleyway on the side of the property.

Applying the principles of spy-craft, the three Okhrana agents resolved to enter the house from both sides at once.

While Trump went to the front door, the same door he had seen used by Mrs. Saint-Albray, Kougloff and Rossiysky took the alleyway, encumbered by two trash cans and strewn with rubble.

Standing on the threshold, Trump knocked twice on the door. Firmly. Even if he was suspicious, the occupant of the house could not ignore those knocks.

Endless seconds passed. Trump had not considered the possibility that the man who was the leader of the group who had kidnapped them might be gone... He thought that, on balance, it would not change their original plan, but just then, he heard a vague movement behind the door, and he tensed up.

Someone wearing slippers approached the door and, in a muffled voice, asked:

"Who's there?"

"Poshekhonsky," Trump answered.

He used that name because he believed there was some kind connection between Novosibirsk Optical & Mechanical Enterprise (NOMO), and the people he was investigating, just as there had been one between the company and Pavel Zakuski.

He heard a deadlock being released, then a key turned twice, and the door half-opened. Trump brutally pushed it wide, and grabbed the person wearing a dressing gown who stood before him, seizing him by the throat.

Requesón, who'd been slightly wary, wasn't totally surprised by the attack. But the sight of the man whom he believed to be dead, drowned in the tank, or at least, still captive there, petrified him to the point of annihilating his combativeness. He stepped back to try to free himself, putting up minimal, absolutely ineffective, resistance.

In less than two minutes, Trump had knocked him out: first, a blow to the carotid artery, followed by a twisting of the arm to force his opponent to lean forward, and then a second blow to the nape of his neck. Requesón, still held by Trump, crumpled to the floor and lay there.

Trump carefully closed the door. A low wattage light bulb spread a pale, bland light along the corridor.

The American waited, his ears attuned to the slightest sound, which, coming from upstairs, might announce the presence of another person, man or woman.

After a minute, he silently walked towards the rear of the ground floor and saw the silhouette of Kougloff trying to look inside the house through the polished glass window of the side door.

Trump turned the key in the lock, and let his two collages inside. With a mocking nod, he pointed to the collapsed body of his opponent.

"That's the guy who questioned me last night," he said. "I think he's the boss of the operation."

Kougloff and Rossiysky made approving noises. Their inquiring looks prompted Trump to add:

"Rossiysky, stay here with him while we check the rest of the building. There may be other people to take care of."

Kougloff nodded.

The two Okhrana agents searched the store, the rest of the ground floor, then the two stories and the cellar without seeing another soul.

Knowing that they were the sole occupants of the house, they dropped their precautions. Requesón was taken back to what they presumed was his bedroom, dropped onto the bed and tied up, while Rossiysky, his stomach twisted in knots, began looking for food.

CHAPTER XXV

When the Mexican finally opened his eyes, he saw three individuals devouring large ham sandwiches with gusto, while occasionally stopping for a sip of beer.

One of them was sitting on his bed; the second man, his legs dangling, sat on a small table, and the third, Donald J. Trump, was slumped in a chair, intently chewing on his sandwich.

"*Salud!*" Trump said, raising his beer bottle to Requesón, after noticing that their captive had regained consciousness.

"We got bored in your country house," added Rossiysky. "Honestly, the plumbing there needs work."

He was speaking in perfect Spanish, which disconcerted Requesón, as Americans were not known for their linguistic abilities. Moreover, Trump, allegedly working for the CIA, seemed in cahoots with the same two FBI agents who had arrested Mrs. Saint-Albray.

Trump began the interrogation while making gluttonous noises as he continued to chew:

"Last time we talked, you asked me about Pavel Zakuski. Was he going to give the new rhodion transistor he stole from the Russians to you?"

Requesón remained silent. Too many conflicting thoughts rattled around in his brain for him to take adequate stock of the situation. The main fact was that he was a prisoner of people who had no reason to spare him, and who seemed well informed about the activities of his own network.

"Yes," he finally admitted with a note of defiance in his voice.

"Why were you interested in the transistor?" asked Trump.

"I wanted to use it in an experiment."

"You know electronics?"

"Yes."

"What is the formula for calculating the frequency of an oscillating circuit?" asked Kougloff.

The Mexican didn't answer.

"Yet, that's a very basic formula," emphasized Kougloff. "So you know nothing of electronics, and you're lying to us."

"Yeah," said Trump. "What was the rhodion for?"

His voice had hardened. He rubbed the crumbs off his knees and stood up next to the bed. He looked at the helpless Mexican menacingly.

Requesón cleared his throat.

"An electronics firm down here had heard about the capacities of this new transistor," he uttered hoarsely. "It could open new vistas in their field, and they wanted to get their hands on a sample without waiting for mass production to begin. Standard business practice."

"How much were they going to pay you?" Trump asked. "Are you the head of the scientific espionage network that Monique Saint-Albray ran in Los Angeles?"

"Yes," affirmed Requesón with suspicious good will.

"Then why don't you work in full cooperation with the Mexican Imperial authorities? A network like yours would only benefit from strong support by the Ministry of Information."

The prisoner's eyes narrowed.

"I do have their support, and it won't be long until you see it," he squeaked. "You won't get out of here alive without my help."

In claiming this, Requesón sought to guarantee his own safety. The three Okhrana agents understood that, but still tried to unravel how much of his statement was true or false.

"You wouldn't have tried to drown us like kittens if you were working for the Mexican authorities," Trump replied. "Enough lies! What are you really up to? Why did the French kill Zakuski?"

Requesón's eyes widened.

"The French?" he repeated, amazed.

"Yes, the French," said Trump. "Why would they camouflage his murder as an accident? Why would they kill a man who carried out a mission for their allies? The truth is, you're working *against* the Mexican Empire. So what's stopping you from telling us everything?"

Kougloff and Rossiysky, holding their breath, stared alternately at Trump and Requesón. They had just learned things they had not known before, and which made the entire affair in which they were caught up much less ordinary.

Scowling, Requesón avoided Trump's beady gaze.

The American, irritated by his silence, leaned forward, both fists on the bed.

"Do you think that the partitioning of your organization will stop us finding out more?" he said. "You're going to tell us what we want to know, by force if necessary. First, what happened to the first man who was following Mrs. Saint-Albray?"

"I don't know," growled the Mexican, stubbornly.

Trump grabbed the back of his robe and gave him two resounding slaps; Then, he grasped the man by the hair, shook his head viciously from left to right, and twisted his ear mercilessly. Requesón squealed in agony.

Trump slammed a pillow over the man's face with one hand, while with his other he twisted Requesón's thumb. The finger, almost at the breaking point, caused an inhuman howl of pain that was barely muffled by the pillow.

Requesón struggled to remove the pillow that choked him.

"No... believe me... I do not know... where your friend is..." he rattled. "Probably in jail... or at the consulate.... It's not my fault.... Quite the contrary..."

"What consulate?" Trump insisted without reducing the pressure.

"The French Consulate. Unless he was handed over to the DIS."

Kougloff and Rossiysky exchanged puzzled looks with Trump.

"How was he taken?" asked the latter.

"We knew Saint-Albray was being followed, but we didn't know by whom. Obviously we weren't the only ones wondering. The French discovered your colleague following her and grabbed him."

Astonished, Trump asked:

"So The French were keeping an eye on her?"

Requesón nodded.

There was a moment of silence. Then Rossiysky broke in:

"He's lying! The French don't care about us! He's making up stories to avoid admitting that they killed Kostromskoy! Let me beat a confession out of him!"

He rushed to the prisoner's side and dealt him two blows to the face that sounded like the crack of a bat on a baseball.

"Calm down," Trump said, after granting him the momentary satisfaction of venting his anger. "Don't knock him out, or we won't get the rest of the story."

His lips bloody, Requesón looked at Rossiysky with hatred.

"Your friend is an idiot," he uttered. "I told you the truth... If your colleague had fallen into my hands, you would have found his body in the tank."

Trump wanted to continue the interrogation undisturbed, and in order to get rid of Rossiysky without alienating him, he suggested:

"Rossiysky, search the house and see if there are any documents or weapons hidden somewhere. We need concrete evidence, or we'll never understand this whole mess."

The Okhrana agent, having recovered his composure, straightened his jacket and replied:

"OK! But when you're tired, let me take over. He still needs to pay for what his two thugs did to us."

"He will, don't worry," Trump promised.

Rossiysky cast a last murderous glance at Requesón before leaving the room.

CHAPTER XXVI

"So the French were also interested in Monique Saint-Albray?" Donald J. Trump asked Requesón in a less aggressive tone.

"Yes. And now, that surprises me even more, since you claim that they're the ones who killed Zakuski."

He looked completely sincere, but still, Trump wondered why that monitoring had miraculously ceased when he and his colleagues had taken over...

"If you suspected that Mrs. Saint-Albray's movements were tracked by the French, why did you call her back here? It doesn't make any sense," asked Trump.

"But I didn't call her; she came on her own."

"Still, you must have been expecting her, since that's how your two thugs caught me?"

The Mexican shrugged.

"They weren't expecting *you*."

Trump had the feeling he was going in circles; an essential clue still escaped him.

Since the beginning, this whole business had been a mess of paradoxical information. Among other things, he couldn't conceive that a spy network, even a private one, could be comprised, in total, of a single informant (Mrs. Saint-Albray), a single liaison officer (Zakuski), a boss cloistered at home in a photo shop (Requesón), and two killers, whose role was not justified in terms of trafficking secret technical information.

"What about Poshekhonsky?" he asked.

"What about him?"

"He went to Zakuski's condo in Los Angeles. You opened the door thinking I was him. What's his role in your network?"

Requesón licked his injured lips.

"None. He has nothing to do with us. He works for NOMO, a Russian optics manufacturer. He visits me from time to time, because I'm a client of his firm."

"And you would just expect him to drop in on you before dawn?"

"We're friends," replied the Mexican.

Trump chewed his lower lip.

Requesón was clever. He excelled at the art of providing plausible answers while revealing practically nothing useful. And most likely, he'd mingled in a few true details with less verifiable ones.

"What happened to Mrs. Saint-Albray?" asked Trump, his eyes half-closed.

"No idea," replied Requesón. "All I know is that she's not at the Hilton any longer."

"That, I already figured out," said Trump. "What I need to know is where she is now. And you're going to tell me, or I'll force it out of you."

The Mexican fell silent. After a few seconds, Trump spoke in a wheedling tone:

"Listen, you're assuming that we're Americans and either can't or won't do anything to you, but you're wrong: we're Okhrana agents."

"Russians?" said Requesón, his eyes widening with fear.

"My two colleagues are. I'm American, but I work with them. We're business partners, you might say. Now, I have two choices: I can either kill you in retaliation for your attempt to murder us, or deliver you straight to the DIS. I'm sure they'll be thrilled to learn of the existence of your organization. Which do you prefer?"

Requesón paled.

"So you see," continued Trump, "I'm putting my cards on the table. We only wanted one thing: to end Saint-Albray's spying activities on Russian businesses. In one way or the other, we've succeeded. Now, you appear to be fighting against the Mexican Empire, and perhaps, we don't really need to destroy your organization. So, I'm offering you a great deal: tell me what I want to know, help me find Mrs. Saint-Albray, and in exchange, I'll let you keep your life and freedom. You have fifteen minutes to think about it. Otherwise, it's *adios muchacho* for you."

Away from the bed, Trump began to wander around the room, looking for a pack of cigarettes. Kougloff watched him. A seasoned spy himself, he appreciated the tactics of his colleague and the results he sought to achieve.

The destruction of an opponent is not always a profitable maneuver; enlisting his cooperation is often a better move, with unsuspected benefits.

Trump unearthed a box of French cigarettes. He offered one to Kougloff before lighting up, using a lighter lying on the nightstand.

Purposefully ignoring Requesón, they began to smoke.

Meanwhile Rossiysky reappeared. He showed them a heavy Remington with a thin barrel, and a magazine located in front of the trigger.

"An excellent nine millimeter weapon, in good condition," he said. "Incidentally, this guy is named Gabriel Requesón, judging by the mail addressed to him. Apart from that, I haven't found anything interesting. It would take a couple of days to search this whole dump."

"Hand me the gun," asked Trump.

Rossiysky handed him the gun and asked:

"Has he talked yet?"

"Not yet, but he's thinking about it. Cigarette?"

The younger Okhrana agent took one eagerly.

Suddenly, Requesón spoke:

"I accept your proposal. However, I would like a guarantee, because I do not have the moral right to tell you everything."

"No guarantees," cut Trump. "Speak first; we'll decide afterwards. If you want to keep mum, that's your business."

Managing to straighten up and lean against the back of the bed, Requesón looked at the three agents, and his eyes dropped involuntarily to the Remington in Trump's hands.

"*Bueno*. My group is only a cell," he finally confessed. "We belong to a rebel movement of democrats that seek to overthrow the Imperial regime. Our work is financed by several industrialists who would like to see Mexico get away from France and become a Republic, and possibly even join the United States. Our movement, which has ramifications worldwide, cooperates with other underground Republican organizations in France, other European countries, and even Russia, who all share the same goals: free their countries from monarchies and set up Republics. There are the *Jacobins* in France, the *Carboneria* in Italy, the *Federación Anarquista* in Spain, an anti-tsarist group called the *Mensheviks* in Russia. We call ourselves the *Convencionistas* because we support the Convention of Mexicali signed in 1914, that was supposed to transfer the powers of the Emperor to the Prime Minister and the Chamber of Deputies, before Eulalio II reneged and dissolved the Government."

He paused, waiting for a sign of approval or disbelief on the faces around him, but they all remained impenetrable.

"Yes, I can understand that you find this odd. We have contacts in Paris, Moscow, Madrid, Rome, Berlin, London, and most of the other European capitals," he continued in a flat voice. "Our primary battlefield is here, in Mexico, but we trade technological advances across national borders. Pavel Zakuski was one of us. He belonged to the *Mensheviks*. They kept us reliably informed of your scientific progress, hence the episode with the rhodion transistor."

For Trump, this was a gold mine of information. It explained why a spy had stolen an object which was not secret or slated for military production. And as a bonus, he had unearthed information on a rebel group operating within Russia that Stroganoff would very much want to hear about.

Requesón continued: "I have no reason to hide that that transistor particularly interested a Mexican firm specializing in infrared applications, which finances us, and which hoped, thanks to the rhodion, to significantly increase the sensitivity of its own infrared detectors..."

"Infrared technology," said Trump. "I suppose they're the ones who provided you with your communications equipment. And that's also how you communicate with your superiors?"

Taken aback by the American's knowledge, Requesón admitted:

"Yes... I guess you found their telescope at Zakuski's? And that's where you met Poshekhonsky?"

"That's right," Trump agreed. "Keep talking!"

CHAPTER XXVII

"I had a secret rendezvous with Zakuski," said Requesón. "When I arrived, I saw the tail lights of a car speeding away towards the highway, and Zakuski's body was in the road. They'd run him over—a Tijuana Tango. I called the police anonymously, and they notified NOMO of his accidental death, but I knew his death was no accident. In fact, I still don't see how the French managed to identify him. It's still a mystery to me, and therefore extremely worrying."

"I can't answer that for you," said Donald J. Trump, "but I can guarantee you that he Russians weren't involved."

Requesón, uncertain, shook his head.

"Then what triggered your own investigation?" he asked Trump, really curious to learn how the grain of sand had interfered with his own plans.

"I would tell you if our roles were reversed," Trump said, with a vague smile on his lips. "Now, tell me about Monique Saint-Albray. What's her story?"

"She's French. Why do you care?"

"She's also American, by marriage. Besides, I want to understand certain obscure details of her behavior that don't entirely fit with what you've told me."

"You know her maiden name is Monique Boursin…"

"Yeah, I do."

"Well, her family were fervent *Jacobins*. Her father was the notorious General Boursin, who was executed during the Algerian Troubles. She hates the Napoleonic regime, which is why she agreed to help us."

"Where is she now? And don't give me a fake address, because if I can't find her, you're the one who'll be sorry."

"We put her up at the Hotel Adria in Ensenada," said Requesón, dejected. "But she won't be there for long. We've made plans to exfiltrate her to Brazil."

Kougloff, surprisingly, tilted his head to one side on hearing this.

"The Adria?" he said, abruptly. "That's patronized by lots of French diplomats. It's where they go to relax when they want a break from Mexico City."

Two seconds later, he added, *mezzo voce*, to Trump:

"We have an agent in place. Just like the French probably had at the Hilton."

A scheme formed in Trump's mind.

"Could you send urgent instructions to your agent?" he inquired in the same tone.

"Not before morning, though."

Trump meditated, then, he turned to Requesón:

"Your thugs stole my passport. Do you still have it?"

The Mexican nodded.

"Where is it?"

"In the left pocket of my overcoat, the one hanging on the coat rack in the hallway."

Trump nodded to Rossiysky. The latter walked out, and soon returned holding the passport, which he handed to Trump.

"OK, it seems we're done for now," Trump said. "We'll untie you, but you're still going to have to put up with us for another few hours. Your, er, guesthouse wasn't very cozy, so we're pretty tuckered out. Besides, we need to look a little more presentable before we go back out. We'll hold up our deal with you, provided, of course, that you refrain from any hostile action towards us, and that you don't try any dirty tricks if your accomplices come back here before we leave."

So saying, he tapped the Remington in the palm of his left hand.

"I don't want to draw attention to my home," grumbled Requesón. "Believe me, there's nothing I want more than for you to get out of here as soon as possible."

For once, he was sincere.

CHAPTER XXVIII

The next day, Donald J. Trump, now back at the Hilton, had breakfast in his room with Kougloff.

The morning paper was spread out on the table. A banner headline read:

TERRORIST ATTACK
Imperial Mexican Airline Flight 057 shot down by missile.

Trump had read the article while he was taking a hot morning bath in the tub, and his brow was still furrowed by the scope of the disaster.

The tone of the article reflected the dismay and concern of the Mexican journalist:

Then followed a statement of facts: a Latécoère 915 aircraft taking off in the middle of the night from Cuauhtemoc International Airport had been shot down by a ground-to-air missile.

The flight carried a delegation of Mexican scientists going to France to discuss their progress in the development of interplanetary vehicles with their French colleagues. It had been hit by a ground-to-air missile mere minutes after take off, while flying over the southern outskirts of Tijuana.

The affair was even more tragic, because many of those who had died in the crash were leading Mexican researchers, specialists known worldwide.

The Mexican investigation was underway. A particularly disturbing rumor was that the missile was reported to have been of French origin.

Kougloff, who had dressed in an elegant outfit, looked depressed.

"This is not good, not good at all," he muttered.

Trumped puffed out his cheeks.

"Very unfortunate indeed. Especially coming so soon after the bomb attack on the French scientists in Pasadena last week. It even looks like retaliation."

Kougloff, anxious, replied in an almost unintelligible voice:

"Do you think Requesón's group is responsible?"

"I do. If the *Convencionistas* want to succeed with their Mexican revolution, they've got to drive a wedge between the two Empires. Rekindle the old enmities that festered after the Great War. What better way to do that than by stoking mutual suspicions about terrorist attacks? That way, the French won't rush to Agustin III's help. Makes perfect sense."

"*Détente* was going too well. We thought that they would cease their bullshit, and here it's starting all over again!"

"What do you want?" sighed Trump. "Life would be too simple if people just gave up on violence. We're not going to be retiring any time soon. Now, what do you have to report?"

"Mrs. Saint-Albray is, indeed, staying at the Adria in Ensenada, room 72," confirmed Kougloff. "I talked to our agent there, and he'll remain there on watch until you arrive. Also, I've gotten you more money to replace what Requesón's thugs stole…"

He inserted a hand into his inside pocket, pulled out a well-stocked wallet and offered it to Trump.

"Dollars. Mexican Francs, it's all there."

"Thanks," Trump said. "Have you sent a status update to Stroganoff?"

"*Da*. You're cleared to go ahead with the operation. He's concerned, too."

Trump got up and shook hands with Kougloff.

"I'll keep you informed, I promise," he said. Thanks and goodbye. My best to Rossiysky."

The two men left the premises of the luxurious Hilton Hotel. Kougloff went to take the subway to return home, while Trump headed down to the rent-a-car desk in the underground parking garage to pick up the brand new Ford Diamante he had reserved the night before.

The drive to Ensenada would take about two hours if he drove leisurely, which he was planning to do, having decided to enjoy himself.

CHAPTER XXIX

The Adria Hotel was located on a large avenue near the waterfront on Boulevard Cabrillo.

Everything was perfectly arranged, as was to be expected from a palace. Comfort, trained staff, and a cozy atmosphere were the hallmarks of the hotel.

Donald J. Trump left his car with the valet, checked in and obtained a room on the third floor. There, he undid his bag, hung his coat in the closet, smoked a cigarette on the balcony, looking at the Pacific, then went back inside and picked up the phone.

"Room 72," he asked the operator.

"*Si señor*," said the employee in an unctuous tone.

Two clicks, then a ring. Someone picked up.

"Hello?" asked the pleasant voice of Monique Saint-Albray.

"Good morning, my dear," Trump said in a cheerful tone. "I've just arrived in Ensenada and I'm looking forward to seeing you. How about right now?"

There was a long silence. Then, the young woman, clearly on the defensive, asked:

"Who is this?"

"Don't you recognize my voice? Not nice! I don't want to spoil the surprise, if you don't. Don't go away. I'll be right there."

He hung up, quickly left the room, carefully locking the door behind him, although he didn't have any illusions about security. A few minutes later, he was knocking on the door of Room 72

It opened and he entered before being invited inside.

Wearing an olive green velvet dress tied at the waist with a white belt, Mrs. Saint-Albray leveled a look at the intruder that managed to be both suspicious and haughty at the same time. Her blond hair looked iridescent under the morning light entering through the large French window framed by heavy dark curtains.

"I've been wanting to talk to you for quite some time," Trump said with an ambiguous smile, while Mrs. Saint-Albray stared at his pale blue piggish eyes.

He closed the door behind her, and observed the woman he had been hunting for nearly a fortnight.

"You must be confusing me with someone else," Mrs. Saint-Albray uttered coldly, yet in a tone that could not hide her apprehension. "What is the meaning of this farce?"

Trump pulled out his silver cigarette case.

"I wonder," he whispered, inserting a cigarette in the corner of his mouth, "what excuse you gave Requesón to justify your refusal to return to Los Angeles?"

Mrs. Saint-Albray's eyelids opened wide and her face suddenly expressed intense anxiety. Involuntarily, she put her clenched fist to her mouth.

"You're mad," she whispered, looking almost haggard. "Don't you know that…"

Her eyes indicated the walls and the ceiling in a frantic warning that they might be monitored.

"Yes, I do," said Trump, taking out his lighter and lighting up his cigarette. "Don't you think that a walk along the harbor would do us a great deal of good? You look peaky."

She stared at him, trying to assess his character, his weaknesses, his vulnerabilities. Also she tried to guess his motives, what had prompted his visit, and what threat he represented.

But he was a man. A bumbling American. She knew she had weapons she could use against him.

"Why go out?" she questioned, her voice recovering part of her initial coolness. "Even though you're mistaken, I'll gladly have a chat with you... Can I offer you a drink?"

"With pleasure," accepted Trump.

He admired her graceful swaying as she headed toward a coffee table in a corner of the room.

Grabbing a beautiful decanter made of Bavarian crystal, she poured two glasses of vodka, took them, and handed one to Trump.

Amused, the American thought that she was now trapped in his net and could no longer escape. Playing a game of cat and mouse with her, in these conditions, titillated him.

Mrs. Saint-Albray raised her glass to Trump.

"*Salud*!"

He responded to her gesture and took a sip as she emptied her glass in one gulp.

"Perhaps my memory is at fault after all," she said. "Did you ever attend one of my *soirées* in Los Angeles?"

"I'm sorry that you don't remember me better," said Trump, playing with her. "Usually, I make more of an impression on women. I haven't forgotten a single detail

150

of your beautiful home; especially that lovely picture of yours that sits in your bedroom..."

A brief flash of recognition lit Mrs. Saint-Albray's eyes.

"Surely our... intimacy... can't have gone that far," she murmured, half opening her moist lips. "But maybe I'm wrong...?"

She approached him, placed her hands around his neck, and looked up at him, her angelic face very close to his brutish one.

"I would do anything if you agreed to, er, forget me afterward," she whispered. "In a couple of hours, I could leave this hotel and be out of reach, anywhere in the world... You could tell your employers that it was bad luck that you missed me..."

Trump gently took her by the waist.

"Unfortunately, my memory is the best memory, and your, er, charms could only serve to sharpen it more," he assured her with a cryptic bonhomie. "But such a sacrifice may not be necessary."

She pulled back, surprised by his almost friendly attitude, the insight of his penetrating eyes and his expression half-mocking, half-understanding.

Against all reason, against all logic, she suddenly felt the desire to trust him, confide in him, snuggle into his arms. She tried to regain her composure, and overcome her strange compulsion.

"I... You... Who are you?" she stammered, as her fingers clutched at his shoulders.

"Take my advice," he insisted, "and let's go out. There's a stifling atmosphere in this hotel."

"Where are you taking me?" she asked worriedly, torn between the spell he had over her and the fear he inspired.

"Let's walk alongside the harbor."

Distraught, Mrs. Saint-Albray dropped her hands. Her brow relaxed.

"Very well, I'll go with you," she surrendered softly.

He released her, and took her hand.

"Don't do anything foolish," he whispered in her ear. "Despair is never a good adviser."

She looked at him perplexed, as if she were hoping to read his thoughts, but saw only a closed face, full of male brutality.

She went to get her coat, put it on quickly, checked in the mirror of her purse to see if her lipstick needed to be touched up, and fixed a few drooping curls of hair.

Finally ready, she asked:

"Should we be seen together?"

"Why not?" Trump replied. "In fact, let's have dinner tonight in the restaurant downstairs."

Unable to discern his true intentions, she shrugged and walked toward the door.

CHAPTER XXX

Donald J. Trump refrained from discussing the heart of the matter until they had reached the concrete square with the statue of Antonio Melendres.

"Just so you know," he began, "I'm the guy who was shadowing you two days ago when you took the train to Rosarito, and who your two friends took prisoner."

"They're not my friends," Mrs. Saint-Albray spat. "They raped me."

"I'm not surprised," he said. "Mexicans are all rapists and murderers. Very bad people. Anyway, they tried to kill me in that abandoned restaurant in Camino Verde, and I was lucky to get out of alive. If I see them again, they'll pay dearly for that, believe me."

"Shoot them—two bullets in the balls. For me," she said, with bitter hatred.

"I will; you can trust me on that. Then, last night, I had a serious discussion with Requesón, who gave me your new address. That's how I found you. Now, what I'd like to know first is if you ratted out Pavel Zakuski to the French?"

Mrs. Saint-Albray stopped. Distraught, she stared at Trump.

"I didn't!" she replied in a quivering voice

"But you work for the French sometimes too," Trump said, acerbic. "And so did your late husband. Not to mention that that missile which destroyed the IMA flight is apparently French-made. Did you provide it to Requesón's group?"

In seconds, Mrs. Saint-Albray realized that this man was not only aware of everything that had happened recently, but he knew her role as a double agent. She had partly guessed this from what he'd first said after entering her room, but now that she knew that Requesón had talked, she felt that it was no longer in her own interest to lie.

"I didn't rat out Zakuski," she repeated. "I think he died because he delayed a job he was supposed to do by one day."

She was no longer denying that she was moonlighting for the French secret service. Trump hardly had to push her for a full confession.

"Tell me what happened," the American said. "I don't need to stress that you're in a very bad situation, and generally, this kind of mistake ends up with an unmarked grave. Believe me, I'm the only one still able to save your skin. So if you want to live, tell me the whole truth."

Mrs. Saint-Albray looked up.

"I'm French, but I'm also a *Jacobin*, like my father," she said in a proud tone. "As a child, I experienced the atrocities of the war in Algeria. He was executed by the Imperials when he tried to help the rebels. I ended up in a refugee camp, before I was allowed to come to the U.S. You need to walk a mile in my shoes before you can judge my conduct."

"Hey, I hate refugees, but I'm not judging," said Trump. "I'd already guessed some of that. But let's go in order: start with that rhodion business."

Despite the warmth, Mrs. Saint-Albray shivered inside her coat. Her hands in her pockets, her small handbag under her arm, she began to walk along the quay.

"That wasn't the beginning, more like the end," she said, staring at the ground. "My late husband was a secret *Jacobin*, too. That's why his family had fled France to emigrate to the United States after the Great War. We hosted many important visitors, businessmen and scientists, at our table. It was after his death that it all started. I was visited by a Spaniard who had been in the same refugee camp as I. A great man! He asked me if I would lend my support to a democratic movement that sought to liberate Mexico from the Habsburgs' rule. Of course, I accepted immediately."

"Why on Earth would you do that? Democracies are for suckers. Look at what the French did with their own Republic, until they saw the light. They and the Russians wouldn't be the great powers they are today without their respective Empires. And Mexico hasn't done too badly either. Sometimes I wish we Americans were smart enough to throw out those do-nothings in Washington and get a real monarch…"

"Well, I don't agree," she replied testily. "But being a lonely rich widow, I welcomed something to avenge me and my father."

Trump understood. One of the reasons he hated refugees, or "Displaced Persons," was because he knew that their camps turned their residents into rebels, anarchists and future shadow fighters. He also thought they were stupid for being losers, on the wrong side of History.

"At first," Mrs. Saint-Albray continued, "I was merely a discreet propagandist; I collected money for the cause, and tried to enlist other refugees living in the United States. Then, after Fernando IV suppressed the Chiapas uprising and hardened his regime, my covert actions took a more active dimension. I helped the *Convencionistas* to connect with like-minded movements in Europe who could help them win their freedom."

"Why Mexico?"

"Because we felt the time was ripe. Since Independence from France, the country has been rife with corruption. Each Habsburg Emperor is more incompetent than the last one. We found many allies in the business community. The cutting edge information I provided helped many Mexican companies to become more competitive, and they, in turn, bankrolled our efforts. And there's the example of the United States to the North. Our plans were proceeding well, until Colonel Roquefort…"

Until then, she had just confirmed Requesón's story. However Trump blinked on hearing these last two words, and he broke in:

"Colonel Roquefort?"

"Yes. As you guessed, I played the part of a double agent, and occasionally provided him with information about what the U.S. scientists were doing, which was worthless to us, but valuable to his government. During one of our clandestine meetings, he let it slip that the new Emperor, Agustin III, is going to negotiate a new free trade agreement with the French, one that would, in effect, again relegate Mexico to the status of semi-colony. So, since we are too weak to overcome the regime by the force of arms, we decided to stop that agreement and torpedo any such initiative by driving a powerful wedge between France and Mexico."

"Would you have gone as far as starting another war?" Trump asked.

"Yes, I would have," replied Mrs. Saint-Albray.

By now their walk had taken them to Ventana al Mar, and they decided to stop at a café-bistro. Trump ordered a coke and she a tea with a slice of lemon.

"Tell me more about your relationship with Colonel Roquefort?" Trump asked.

"Honestly, it was Requesón's idea. The best way to be informed about the French intentions towards Mexico was to introduce a double-agent into their own service. Los Angeles was, in this regard, an ideal post. To get myself recruited by Roquefort wasn't difficult; I had everything I needed to entice him: an unassailable social position, valuable relationships with many local scientists, and a Francophile past. He welcomed me with open arms. But in reality, I watched them more than I was giving them information."

"Still, as you said, the information you got from all those scientists at your *soirées*, proved very useful to them."

"Of course! I had to justify my role! That is the painful side of being a double-agent, as you must know. You can't help but assist your enemy. Thus, with respect to the rhodion transistor, I gave the same information I'd gotten from Ramon Bandel to Roquefort and Pavel Zakuski, but I'd told Zakuski a day earlier in order for him to have the time..."

As she hesitated, Trump finished her sentence:

"...To get a prototype from Louie Ragusano's factory in Burbank. And I assume that the French agents, who sought to do the same, spotted him there?"

"I suppose some coincidence like that must have happened," Mrs. Saint-Albray agreed sullenly.

Now Trump understood the actions of the French and Roquefort's ulterior motives during their earlier conversation.

When he had become aware of Zakuski's actions, Roquefort had thought he was dealing with a Mexican spy, but what he didn't know was if Zakuski was somehow connected to their old enemy, the Russians, whom he thought were eager to sow trouble in Mexico.

In order to find out, he had had Zakuski followed all the way down to Tijuana, and there, had had him coldly eliminated. Afterward, he had brought the rhodion to the attention of the Okhrana in order to test the Russians' good faith.

At no point had the French spymaster realized that Zakuski was, in fact, working together with their own informer, who was secretly a Democrat seeking to overthrow the Mexican Imperial regime!

CHAPTER XXXI

"So, why did you come to Tijuana?" Donald J. Trump asked.

Mrs. Saint-Albray looked at him obliquely. It was clear he wanted to know every detail.

"Requesón contacted me through Poshekhonsky to tell me about Zakuski's death. He decided to move ahead of schedule faster than planned…"

"You mean, the Pasadena bombing?"

"Yes. He thought that, if the French were on to Zakuski, and that they discovered the Russians weren't involved in all of it, they would begin to suspect the existence of our movement. My position would suddenly become dangerous, and our plan to drive a wedge between the two countries would fall apart. So we had to move quickly. Poshekhonsky arranged for the Pasadena bombing, then sent a message to warn me and fled to Mexico."

Trump gave a low whistle of admiration,

"He sure was efficient. I'd never have guessed it from meeting him. So what did you do?"

"We had an old French ground-to-air missile that my husband had acquired a long time ago from some arms trafficker; it was stored in one of our refineries in

San Diego. It was child's play to get it transferred across the border to Mexico inside a fuel truck."

Trump's blood ran cold.

"And that's what Requesón used to shoot down Flight 057?"

"Yes," she said, lowering her eyes.

"But what about Roquefort? He just let you go, like that?" asked Trump, snapping his fingers.

"No. I had to make up a story. I told him I was on the trail of the people behind the Pasadena bombing. He was happy to believe me. And really, I was telling him the truth," she snickered. "*We* were the people behind the bombing."

"What happened then?"

"I went down to Tijuana and stayed at the Hilton. Roquefort sent two of his men to shadow me. It didn't take them long to realize someone else was also following me, so they took him prisoner and interrogated him."

So that's what had happened to Kostromskoy!

"They reported to me after I returned to the Hilton," Mrs. Saint-Albray continued in a voice tinged with bitterness. "After what had happened to Zakuski, I had reason to be worried... I didn't know who else, other than the French could have been monitoring my activities. And then, I found out that the Americans were after me!"

"Why? Because Kostromskoy told them he was an American agent?"

"Yes. CIA—just like you," she said, mildly puzzled.

Trump let the statement stand without comment.

"What did Roquefort do then?"

"He thought I'd been on a wild goose chase, because the Americans clearly had nothing to do with the

Pasadena bombing. Their services have been infiltrated by both Russian and French intelligence for decades. They can't lift a finger without Paris or Moscow hearing about it."

Trump smiled, but said nothing.

"Roquefort called off his men, but I noticed I was still being followed. I was really concerned, so I decided to notify Requesón. I deliberately set myself up as bait. I went down to his shop in Rosarito, knowing that he would set up some kind of countermeasure. So you're the one those two scum bags Alfredo and Manuel caught?"

"Yes. Requesón even seemed a little embarrassed when I told him that I worked for the CIA. He was probably confused by the fact that we were on your tail too... But when you discovered that you were burned in Los Angeles, how come you sought to hide out here? And what were you going to tell the French to explain your refusal to return to Los Angeles?"

Mrs. Saint-Albray shrugged wearily.

"Nothing. Requesón is the one who booked me a room at the Adria, where his organization has several agents. I worried he would throw me to the wolves, but over the years, he's grown to like me. He's arranged for me to flee to Brazil."

"Brazil is better than two bullets in the head," Trump nodded.

Based on what he'd just learned from both Mrs. Saint-Albray and Requesón, Trump knew that Kostromskoy had been taken by the French; but Russia could not tolerate their further interference in Mexico's business. Therefore, it was necessary for the *Convencionistas*' plan to fail.

They had finished their drinks. Trump looked inquiringly at Mrs. Saint-Albray.

"What's the rest of Requesón's plan?" he asked, taking his cigarettes from his pocket. "Tell me. I need to know everything. Your life depends on it."

Mrs. Saint-Albray grew even paler. She murmured:

"Tomorrow night, friends of ours in the media—not just in Mexico, but in your country as well—will reveal that they have evidence that the bomb that killed the French rocket scientists in Pasadena was planted by a rogue unit of Mexican intelligence, and the French retaliated by shooting down Flight 057. Relations between the two countries will break down; maybe worse. It will be the death knell of the Mexican Empire. Without France's support, they'll never survive."

"When is this news release planned to happen?"

Her eyes fixed straight ahead, she replied:

"8 p.m. New York time; that's 5 p.m. Los Angeles. But why do you want to stop us? If the Empire collapses and Mexico does become a Republic, your country will benefit too."

She meant the United States. Trump smiled. She'd find out soon enough where his true loyalties lay.

"Perhaps, but public opinion will heat up on both sides of the fence, like your group hopes, and if Requesón considers a rain of fire and blood a small price to pay for bringing down the Imperial regime, personally, I prefer a peaceful world to one ravaged by war."

A dull irritation filled his voice, though his expression remained unchanged. However, he had inserted his arm under Mrs. Saint-Albray's and he led her back to the Adria.

"What are you going to do?" she asked, consumed with anxiety.

"First, take you back to the hotel, where you will wait for me without moving an inch and without communicating with anyone. If you obey my instructions, I'll let you flee to Brazil and good riddance. But if you try to stab me in the back remember that I can have you in the hands of the DIS in a matter of minutes. Now, I have to pay another visit to your boss…"

CHAPTER XXXII

At four in the afternoon, Donald J. Trump was back at the Hilton, and three hours later, as dusk fell and the street lights were coming on, he entered Requesón's photo store in Rosarito.

The Mexican's eyes widened at the sight of him. In his right hand, Trump held the Remington he had seized that morning, while he locked the door behind him with the other.

"Step into the back room and no funny business," he ordered.

Requesón protested:

"But, you promised that..."

"Keeping promises is for chumps. Come on, hurry up!"

Requesón, subdued, obeyed. He knew that his life was in the balance.

They both walked into a room with a desk and some inventory. The *Convencionista* leader, distraught, looked at his visitor with anguish.

"Didn't you see Mrs. Saint-Albray? Wasn't she at the Adria?" he asked, his mouth dry.

"Yeah, I saw her," said Trump, "and she revealed a few points that you seem to have forgotten to mention to me. In particular, that it was you who ordered her to act as a double agent for the French, and that your battlefield, as you yourself put it, isn't just a peaceful revolution, but setting fire to the entire Western hemisphere in the name of your crazy democratic delusions... You're stepping on a lot of corpses doing that..."

Requesón's Adam's apple bounced up and down.

"I didn't lie to you," he gasped, mesmerized by the barrel of the gun pointed at his stomach.

"No, but you didn't tell me the whole truth either. No matter. What I want from you is a full, written confession where you admit your organization's involvement in the circumstances of the Pasadena attack and shooting down Flight 057."

An incredulous grin slowly appeared on the Mexican's face.

"Never in a million years," he said in a broken voice. "I had nothing to do with either event."

"Stop lying. And to be honest, I don't give a rat's ass about either act," Trump said sarcastically. "But you're going to take responsibility for them because you had all the necessary tools, and in addition, you had a motive. I'll take your letter to Colonel Roquefort; he'll be able to check it out, and the French will lay off. They'll send a copy to the DIS and all will go back to normal."

Inwardly, Requesón blamed Monique Saint-Albray, who obviously had spilled more beans than necessary—what an idiot!

His anger stoked his arrogance:

"You can shoot me on the spot if you want, but I won't write a word," he challenged. "Death doesn't scare me. Death to the tyrants!"

"Maybe," admitted Trump. "But I won't shoot you if you don't write that letter. Instead, I'll call Roquefort and hand you over to him. The results will be the same—except worse for you. But if you write me a very detailed and convincing statement, I'll let you disappear in accordance with my promise of this morning. You can go to Brazil and start a new life with Mrs. Saint-Albray, or wherever else you like."

Requesón clenched his jaws. He was beaten. Even if by some miracle he managed to get rid of his opponent, the game was over. Tentatively, he suggested:

"And in exchange for a full confession and all the information about our network, would you consider getting me a refugee visa for the United States?"

"You kidding me? And what else? Making you a Senator?" Trump quipped. "Be happy that I'm willing to let you go instead of turning you in for your crime! Between Flight 057 and the bombing, I'm sure your DIS would invent new forms of torture you can't even dream of! You're lucky that I just don't give a shit. Now, write!"

Sullenly, Requesón grumbled:

"I need to lower my hands first."

"Don't move yet," ordered Trump.

He made sure no weapons were hidden in the desk drawers or in its immediate vicinity.

"OK, now you can sit and write. Start at the beginning, name names, and detail all the facts to provide proof of what you say..."

Bantering, he added:

"Hell! I don't even care if you blame your cohorts for shooting down that plane. What matters is that your testimony is convincing. You sought to reignite the Colonial Wars and I intend to pour a bucket of cold water on it."

While Requesón started to write, Trump went back into the store and a sign on the door that read: "Closed for inventory."

CHAPTER XXXIII

Donald J. Trump returned to the Adria Hotel at 10p.m. He had already sent copies of Requesón's "confession" to Stroganoff by overnight mail.

From the lobby, he telephoned Monique Saint-Albray.

"See you at the bar in fifteen minutes for the appetizers," he said, his mood jovial. "Then we can have dinner."

Mrs. Saint-Albray mumbled her acquiescence; Trump hung up immediately.

She felt buffeted by events beyond her control, and only wanted to spend an evening in pleasant company, even if it was this obnoxious narcissist who held her fate in his tiny hands. It was almost a relief for her to rely entirely on him to decide what her future would be.

They met at the bar, both showing studied indifference towards each other, and chatted about a wide range of topics far removed from their actual concerns. Mrs. Saint-Albray barely touched her food while Trump piggishly ate his third meal of the day.

At the end of dinner, he proposed going back to her room. She understood that her dinner companion was in no hurry to send her to a Mexican dungeon and her mood brightened a little. Fatalistic, like all ex-refugees, she wished to drown herself in the pleasures of the moment in order to forget the past and not think about the future. So she agreed. And she was strangely physically attracted to the man. She also took a certain interest in studying his behavior.

Trump mistook her compliance as his due. He made neither a gesture nor word that could have been construed as a gallant afterthought. He knew what he wanted; he just took it.

A short while later, as he dressed, he changed his tone to address their common problems.

"I've had time to think since this afternoon," he stated. "I think being on the run in Brazil isn't necessarily the best option for someone with your, er, talents."

"I see," said Mrs. Saint-Albray. "Or at least, I think I do. But I would prefer that you tell me clearly what you're offering me..."

"To reclaim your previous situation. It's the only way for you to preserve all the things you cherish. Obviously, you'll have to give up the cause you fought for... Besides, it's a lost cause..."

In the darkness, Mrs. Saint-Albray glanced questioningly at Trump.

"Have you seen Requesón?" she asked.

He nodded. "He's probably on the run by now, and I suppose he must have sent some kind of alarm signal to his network to scuttle it. At least, I would have. Too bad for the others if he didn't. One thing for sure, we won't tolerate these sorcerer's apprentices continuing to play with matches in a powder keg. So, are you willing to come and work for us?"

Mrs. Saint-Albray remained silent. Not because she hesitated over her decision, but because she secretly relished returning to Los Angeles.

"Yes," she finally responded with a Mona Lisa smile. "But what task do you have in mind for me?"

"It's not my job to decide that," replied Trump, "but I imagine my superiors will want you to continue playing double-agent with the French, and provide us with all that you learned about these democratic terrorist networks, so we can assess their importance, their penetration of our own institutions, and the leaks for which they're responsible. And of course, we'll want you to continue with your *soirées* and provide us with the valuable scientific information you collect there."

Mrs. Saint-Albray reflected, then she remarked:

"But if I remain free, don't you think the French will be suspicious? They'll find out who I had dinner with... Trace you back to the CIA..."

"Ah, but you see, baby, I don't work for the CIA," Trump said, smiling.

Her eyes widened under the effect of this revelation. "You don't?" she said. "But then, who...?"

"Of course, the French will know that you're a double agent," Trump continued. "Colonel Roquefort isn't stupid. They won't care. They can still get a lot of valuable information from you. As far we're concerned, crushing these democratic bastards is going to be one cause we'll have in common, for sure. But to answer your question, I'm moonlighting for the Russians."

As Mrs. Saint-Albray curiously turned over in her mind the notion of becoming a Russian agent, he added, chuckling:

"I'll introduce you to my handler, Boris Fedorovitch Stroganoff. I'm sure you'll get along great!"

CHAPTER XXXIV

Donald J. Trump met with Colonel Roquefort the next afternoon at the French Consulate on Sunset Boulevard.

As before, the colonel greeted the emissary of the Okhrana with sincere cordiality.

"What good wind brings you back here, Mr. Trump?" he asked after inviting his visitor to sit, then offering him a cigar box. "Are you still bothered by that small matter of the stolen rhodion transistor?"

"Not at all," replied Trump, casually. "Quite the contrary, I came to inform you, as a *quid pro quo*, that we discovered the existence of a network that, while primarily operating out of Mexico, tried to sabotage the peaceful coexistence between that country and France, a matter obviously totally unrelated to the stolen rhodion issue."

The cordial expression on Roquefort's face suddenly vanished, to be replaced by hardened concern.

"Go on," he muttered, looking darkly at his visitor.

Trump shook his head in assent.

"Our Mexican agents got wind of the whole thing... They gathered a lot of information about that organization, the *Convencionistas*, and sent us a file. However, as this matter concerns you more than us, geographically speaking, my superiors thought it best to make you aware of the problem."

Roquefort clasped his hands and leaned his elbows on his desk.

"It interests us mightily, Mr. Trump," he assured gravely. "We know there are those in Mexico who dislike us because they don't understand our Emperor's intentions, but we thought that enough water had flowed under the bridge, and old disagreements had been ironed out. We can't allow a handful of democratic fanatics to undermine world peace, can we? You said you can provide us with details about these *Convencionistas'* operations?"

"Certainly. Among other things, I can tell you how and who did the Pasadena bombing and took out Flight 057."

The colonel hiccuped. His body stiffened, his complexion flushed, and he asked in an almost begging voice:

"You know the culprits?"

"Yes. I have names, addresses, all the evidence you need to contact the DIS... Everything is in this folder, which my superiors asked me to give you. Basically, a ground-to-air missile stolen from your arsenal was fired from the roof of an abandoned factory in Tijuana; you'll find the location in the report..."

While talking, he had taken a red folder from his briefcase and absently patted it with his left hand.

Roquefort stared hungrily at it, and had to exercise great restraint to not simply jump up and grab it.

"Holy Mother Russia rendered a great service to the cause of peace, Mr. Trump," he uttered in an emotional voice. "I really do not know how to express the gratitude of the French Empire... We can show the world we had nothing to do with this horrible tragedy and move against the terrorists who are truly responsible for it."

"Absolutely!" Trump said approvingly without moving his hand from the red folder. "Before that can be done, however, we need your help. We're looking for one of our agents who mysteriously disappeared in Tijuana. Would it be possible for you to check if he wasn't taken by the DIS by mistake? We know you carry quite a lot of influence with them. If they have him, we would appreciate his discreet return."

Roquefort armed himself with a notepad and a pen.

"Of course! Tell me the identity of this man," he said decisively, "and I promise you that if he is anywhere in Mexico, I'll have him delivered back to you dead or alive within the week."

Trump consulted a sheet of paper and read aloud the information that was on Kostromskoy's fake ID card, which Kougloff had given him before he'd left Tijuana.

While Colonel Roquefort scrupulously transcribed the information, Trump placed the red folder on his desk.

After leaving the French Consulate, from Sunset Boulevard, Trump drove to Westwood. He entered the condominium building where Pavel Zakuski had lived and took the elevator to the fourth floor. He rang the bell.

A man of about thirty-five, with a square face and prominent jaw, opened the door. He looked at the visitor with a shade of astonishment, then asked in English burdened with a strong Russian accent:

"You wish, Mister…?"

"Are you the new general representative of Novosibirsk Optiko-Mechanichesckoye Obyedinenie?" inquired Trump.

"Yes," nodded the Russian.

He stood aside to let Trump inside the condo.

"I'm not yet fully settled," he said, with an apologetic gesture indicating the disorder that reigned in the room. "I arrived from Novosibirsk only five days ago, and..."

"Don't bother," said Trump, seeing that his host had hastened to dust off a chair. "I just came for a quick chat and to get acquainted, because I knew your predecessor."

"Really? Well... My name is Petru Bryndza."

So saying, he bowed slightly, and extended his outstretched hand.

"Donald. J. Trump. I'm in real estate."

They examined each other for two seconds, then Trump said:

"I assume that, like the late Pavel Zakuski, you're going to focus on increasing revenues and further developing trade with Mexico?"

Bryndza, his face serious, nodded in the affirmative.

"*Da*. It is great honor for me, and I will devote all my time to it," he said with conviction.

Trump, looking pensive, continued in a neutral tone:

"That is an excellent plan, Mr. Bryndza. I would strongly encourage you to follow it without the slightest deviation. It is often dangerous to try to run two businesses simultaneously."

The NOMO representative looked at him with questioning eyes, a vertical wrinkle between his eyebrows deepening.

"What do you mean, two businesses?"

"Simply this: it could happen that a certain Mr. Vladimir Poshekhonsky, or some other ex-employee of NOMO, asks you, in the near future, to help with something other than the sale of photographic equipment. If I can give you a piece of advice, refuse, even if it costs you your job. Such a move could have serious consequences for you."

And not caring of whether the amazement painted on Bryndza's face was feigned or genuine, Trump walked back towards the door.

There, he turned and handed the Russian a card.

"Of course, if you do hear from Mr. Poshekhonsky or someone like him, and you call that number immediately, there will be a substantial reward for you, and you would benefit from strong protection."

He grabbed the handle, and stepped out.

"My suggestion would be for you to burn this card and consign the number to your memory. *Dasvidaniya*, Mr. Bryndza. Enjoy your time in Los Angeles."

Leaving the Russian flabbergasted, he waved him farewell and left.

CHAPTER XXXV

Four days later, Donald J. Trump, after having taken care of some urgent business in his father's organization, returned to the *Little Odessa* restaurant in Brighton Beach to meet with Boris Fedorovitch Stroganoff.

"Damn!" said the Okhrana Director. "I've just received a report from Kougloff, and here you are already... Do you have an update on our pretty new friend?"

"Right now, she's back in L.A.," said Trump, unbuttoning his overcoat. "She took the train just before mine."

"Do you trust her?"

"Of course not. But she was persuaded by my arguments, and we have a lot of leverage on her. Her *soirées* will get us more valuable information, and if you want to convince the French that we're building a new interceptor rocket or a device to turn their wine into piss, she'll be an ideal conduit."

Stroganoff frowned, then muttered:

"You don't think Roquefort is going to have her eliminated?"

Trump smiled.

"I don't think so. He has no reason to kill her. He was obviously unaware that she was a double-agent, and that the guy who'd stolen a rhodion transistor was in league with her and the *Convencionistas*. Now he knows she works for us, but he also realizes that, thanks to her services, he'll be able to get hot tips about any democratic activity in Mexico in the future."

Stroganoff's features relaxed, and he began to rub his hands with satisfaction.

"You know that I always like it when you tell me the whole story yourself, in broad strokes," he invited. "The report Kougloff sent me is thorough, but sketchy on the local flavor. Let's eat, and you can tell me everything..."

While they shared some Shashlyik, Trump proceeded to tell his boss the finer details of the recent operation, and add his insight. After his presentation, he concluded:

"In short, the real villains were those fanatics trying to overthrow our regimes. People like Requesón will have to be watched and rooted out, even here, in America. A country is nothing without a strong leader."

"Requesón... Kougloff mentions him in an update attached at the end of his report... Let me see..."

Stroganoff adjusted his glasses and looked at a sheet of paper.

"There it is... He was run over by a car yesterday in Ciudad del Panama."

"The Tijuana Tango," said Trump smiling.

"The what?"

MODERN FRENCH SF & FANTASY
FROM BLACK COAT PRESS

G.-J. Arnaud. *The Ice Company*
Richard Bessiere. *The Gardens of the Apocalypse* (also includes *The Seven Rings of Rhea*)
Richard Bessiere. *The Masters of Silence* (also includes *They Came From the Dark*)
André Caroff. *The Terror of Madame Atomos*
André Caroff. *Miss Atomos*
André Caroff. *The Return of Madame Atomos*
André Caroff. *The Mistake of Madame Atomos*
André Caroff. *The Monsters of Madame Atomos*
André Caroff. *The Revenge of Madame Atomos*
André Caroff. *The Resurrection of Madame Atomos*
André Caroff. *The Mark of Madame Atomos*
André Caroff. *The Spheres of Madame Atomos*
André Caroff, Michel & Sylvie Stéphan. *The Wrath of Madame Atomos*
André Caroff, Michel & Sylvie Stéphan. *The Sins of Madame Atomos*
Jean-Claude Dunyach. *The Night Orchid*
Jean-Claude Dunyach. *The Thieves of Silence*
Jimmy Guieu. *The Polarian-Denebian War 1: Operation Aphrodite*
Jimmy Guieu. *The Polarian-Denebian War 2: Space Commandos*
Nathalie Henneberg. *The Green Gods*
P.-J. Hérault. *The Clone Rebellion*
Romain d'Huissier: *Hexagon: Dark Matter*
Gérard Klein. *The More in Time's Eye*